CW01430554

THE
PERFECT
MEAL

SUZI WIELAND

Twisted Path Press

Copyright ©2019 by Suzi Wieland

All rights reserved. The reproduction or utilization of this work in whole or in part, by any means, is forbidden without written permission from the author.

This book is a work of fiction. Names, characters, places, and incidents are products of the author's imagination or are used fictitiously. Any resemblance to actual events, locations, or persons, living or dead is entirely coincidental.
Published by Twisted Path Press

Cover by Krafigs Design

First edition September 2019, Second edition May 2022, Third edition July 2024

Chapter One

Just one bite. One bite to make sure the perfectly round meatball tasted as good as it looked.

Camilla bit into the scrumptious ball. It wasn't really stealing. She was the chef after all. Well, maid, not chef, but her maid duties included the cooking.

She finished her taste test and dished up the bowl of meatballs, making sure to check her mouth was free of crumbs. Then she served dinner to Karin and Roald Berdahl and left them to eat.

It's not like she would've gotten in trouble for eating one meatball. In fact, Roald would have probably teased her and said to take more. But they had never actually told her she could eat their food, so she didn't want to get caught.

Camilla waited in the kitchen while the Berdahls finished dinner, happy that it was almost the end of the day.

"Camilla," Karin called from the dining room. "You may clear the dishes now."

THE PERFECT MEAL

Camilla hustled from the kitchen into the other room, her joints aching. The day had been long, spent on her hands and knees scrubbing the floor. As soon as the dishes were done, she could go home, rest, and take a break since she didn't work tomorrow. Sunday was her only day off.

Roald Berdahl held his dirty plate up to her, and she removed it before going to his wife to retrieve hers. The house was quiet with their two kids visiting Roald's mother.

"The meatballs were absolutely perfect," Karin gushed. "I don't know what spices you used, but they were delicious. One day you should consider becoming a chef and catering meals. The Grand Inn needs a better cook."

"A-hem." Roald cleared his throat. "And why are you trying to get rid of the best maid we've ever had?"

Karin giggled and bowed her red face. "You are so right, my dear. Forget I said a thing." She turned to Camilla. "I don't know what I'd do without you."

The words were true. Karin used each and every hour of Camilla's day to its fullest. Not just the cleaning and cooking, but planning activities for her ladies socials: garden parties, rousing games of bridge, and charity events, all opportunities to enjoy a glass of akevitt and conversation with her friends.

"Thank you for the compliment." Camilla wasn't about to walk away from her stable job. Yes, they worked her hard, but they treated her well and always paid her on time, unlike the family her middle sister worked for.

The Pettersens, whose children Marit took care of, rarely paid her when she was due. It was better though with her eldest sister, Hilde, who worked at the school. Despite Camilla and her two older sisters having jobs, money was always short. Hilde really needed to find a job closer to home. The school was a half-hour horse ride, and if they didn't have a horse to care for, they would have more money.

"I will take care of these dishes, and then I'll be leaving." Camilla piled Karin's plate on top of Roald's.

"Thank you, Camilla. We'll see you Monday morning." Karin nodded warmly. "It's time to polish the silver again. I know you love that job."

Camilla didn't really love polishing silver, but what she appreciated was how Karin helped her with the job. They made a morning of it, talking as they worked, and Karin invited Camilla to have a cup of tea after they were done, as if they were friends.

"Oh, I almost forgot to tell you," Roald said to his wife. "I was speaking today with Magnus, and he said they are investigating the boarding school in Horsten."

Camilla's ears perked up, and she slowed down her collecting of dishes. That was the school Hilde worked at.

"Whatever for?" Karin asked.

"Someone's been stealing money. They think it might be the headmaster because there is some trickery going on with the books."

"Oh, that's awful." Karin shook her head disapprovingly.

Camilla had to leave the dining room to bring the china dishes to the kitchen, but she returned quickly to collect the others. She wanted to hear the rest of the story so she could speak to Hilde about it.

"So they're sure there are several others involved?" Karin said.

"Yes, any of them." Roald sighed.

Curses. Camilla had missed some of the other possible suspects.

"I hope they catch the scoundrels." Karin patted her mouth with the cloth napkin. "Camilla, doesn't your older sister teach in Horsten?"

"Yes, she does." Camilla suddenly felt guilty, being associated with such a scandal, which was silly.

"It wouldn't be a teacher," Roald said. "They don't have access to the funds. It has to be an administrator."

Thank goodness. Not that Camilla would suspect Hilde, but other people might scrutinize any and every person who worked at the school.

The remaining dishes were piled in Camilla's hands, and she had no choice but to return to the kitchen. She quickly washed them up, put them away, grabbed her cloak, and made her way down the path to the road. The twenty-minute walk to her home in the woods with her sisters was tiring after a long day, but they had little choice. They could not afford a home in town, and besides, the house was almost paid off.

Their parents died just over two years ago and luckily had not left them with a big loan to the bank. For the home at least.

The sun had dipped beneath the tops of the trees, but darkness had not yet arrived. The frogs and bugs and birds accompanied her, and it was mostly a peaceful walk.

Until a wagon flew past her. She waved to the occupants even though she didn't recognize them and then fingered the old ink stain on her apron. It had faded with time, but no matter what she had done, she couldn't get it out. It was Marit's fault as she had allowed the stain to set. If only she'd attacked it right away, it might not be there.

Finally Camilla hit the dirt tracks to her house. So many times she had wished for a wagon, but they'd had to sell theirs after her mother and father died. He owed money at the builder's shop, and the owner would not cancel the loan after her parents' deaths.

Yes, a wagon would be nice, but then she wouldn't enjoy the quiet solitude of the forest as she did on her walks.

Camilla hesitated in the yard, staring up at the old house. Her father had such grand plans for this home, which had been inexpensive to purchase because it had been in such rough shape. Her parents bought it a few months before they died, with intentions to fix it up and make it more livable, but Father had gotten sick and died, with Mother soon following.

Camilla let the strap of her satchel slip off her shoulder and fall to the ground. She missed her father's hearty laugh and her mother's sweet hugs. The past two years without them had been hard.

After a few more moments, she ascended the steps, avoiding the broken step.

Inside the small kitchen, Camilla stared at the rusty sink full of dirty dishes. Hilde didn't work at the school on Saturdays, and Marit usually got home from her job around four, but Camilla, who was never home until after seven, was always left to clean up after them.

At least they left out some of the roast and potatoes for her to eat. It was dry as usual. No matter how many times Camilla told Hilde what to do, she always cooked the beef too long, usually getting distracted and forgetting about it.

Camilla took the plate of food to the table and sat for a quiet moment before eating. Thank goodness she did not work tomorrow. Of course she had plenty to do around the house, chores to catch up on, and another skirt to sew. Maybe if she were lucky, she could find some time to sit on her favorite swing and write a new story in her book. Her mother had encouraged her with her drawings, but Camilla had never shared the stories she wrote.

The bite of beef was like leather, and Camilla swallowed it down.

Marit and Hilde walked down the steps and plunked down on the sofa, chattering. Neither looked over at Camilla, but she was used to their lack of attention. She was the baby, only eighteen, and her sisters sometimes treated her like she was two.

"I am so tired of those little rascals." Marit leaned back and set her hand over her forehead. Camilla wasn't sure why she complained so much. The oldest Pettersen child was fourteen and the youngest twelve, hardly much work.

"I can't blame you." Hilde shook her head in complete agreement. "You should find a better job in Skaane. It's bigger than Estfold and actually has some decent stores and people. If I wasn't in Horsten, I would work there."

Goodness gracious, Hilde, why are you putting that thought in her head? Only eight hundred people lived in Estfold, and the town was too small for her two sisters, but Skaane was the opposite direction of Horsten and far enough away that Marit would also need a horse.

"I would like to quit, but there's no way that is happening." Marit grinned at Hilde.

Camilla sure hoped Marit wasn't thinking about quitting. They had the house and many of the supplies her father had bought. Those supplies had been forgotten for a time in the barn, the girls unable to use them, and they were ruined by a leak in the roof and couldn't be returned. But they still had to pay for them.

"Did you help Mrs. Pettersen pack?" Camilla asked Marit, and both sisters turned and stared like they hadn't even realized she was there.

"That's not my job." Marit scoffed. "Mrs. Pettersen doesn't require any menial work, thank the stars. My delicate hands can not take that kind of work. And besides, I have enough to do with the children."

Marit's nose wrinkled up. "How did you know she was leaving?"

Because this town is small enough that everybody knows everybody. Camilla held her tongue though, so not to raise her sister's ire. But really, it was the exact reason Marit complained about Estfold.

"She and Karin belong to the women's society."

Mrs. Pettersen had hosted several events at their home, requiring Marit to keep the children out of sight.

"Spectacular news." Marit ran a hand through her curly dark hair. She and Hilde almost looked like twins with their same black hair and blue eyes and statuesque bodies, but they were a full year apart. Camilla, on the other hand, had light brown hair and wore a few too many pounds. "I am working longer hours this week, so I can put more money towards our moving fund."

Camilla kept the smile plastered on her face, but inside she sighed. Her sisters had this silly idea of moving to Trenten to become famous actresses. Trenten had a large university, museums, tall, tall buildings, and thousands and thousands of people.

It wasn't the town Camilla was opposed to though, but the long and dangerous journey to get there. She didn't want to risk her life for a move to an unknown city. They'd know nobody, they'd have no jobs, and they'd have no place to live.

9

A dreamy look crossed Hilde's face. "At the school, they talk of the Hus. It's a grand theater where they have plays and operas. Could you imagine me on stage?" Hilde's voice rose an octave, and she sang a few *la la las*.

Her voice wasn't bad, but Camilla didn't think she had the skills to be cast in a production. In fact, Hilde hadn't even wanted to be a part of the Estfold Theater Troop.

"You can star in the operas, and I will star in the plays and musicals. Good thing I'm talented all around. I might even try out for a ballet." Marit wiggled her shoulders and waved her arms in the air, her whole body swaying.

Camilla hid her laugh. Marit was not smooth on her feet.

Marit turned to Camilla. "You could be a stage hand. Or make costumes."

"Why can't I be on stage too?" Camilla bristled.

"You?" Hilde scoffed, looking down her nose at her youngest sister. "They do not cast chubby leading ladies."

"Yes," Marit said, rolling her eyes. "And how would you learn all the lines? You didn't even finish school."

Because of you, Camilla wanted to say. Her sisters forced her to quit her schooling after her parents died. She could have just worked in the evenings and weekends as she finished her last two years, but they insisted she quit.

Camilla slunk down in her seat. She didn't have the soft curves her sisters did, and she was just as smart as they were, but they didn't have to be so mean about it. When her parents were alive, Hilde and Marit had not been so awful. Or maybe it was that she'd paid less attention because her mom had been warm and loving and her father always the one to make her smile.

"And the Berdahls wouldn't want you to leave," Marit added.

Oh, that reminded Camilla of Roald and Karin's conversation. "Say, they were talking tonight. Roald said your school is opening up an investigation over missing money."

"What?" Hilde's brows shot up, and her back straightened. "What did they say?"

"Roald talked to Magnus—"

"Who's Magnus?"

"Roald's brother. Magnus Berdahl. His kids attend your school. They're older though, so you might not have run into them. But he said that money is missing, and they suspect an administrator, perhaps even the headmaster."

Marit gasped. "Are you serious?"

"Yes, do you have any idea of who it could be?" Camilla asked Hilde. Hopefully they would find the responsible party and arrest them. Hilde often complained about how the school never had enough money for supplies and upkeep on their building.

"Of course not," Hilde snapped. Her head fell, and she stared down into her lap. "It can't be the headmaster. I don't know who it would be. Probably the woman who pays everybody."

"How much money?" Marit asked.

"I didn't hear that, but enough that they're doing an investigation."

"That's awful. How can people steal from children like that? I hope they catch the thieves." Hilde frowned and stood. "Did Marit tell you we're having a party for Tally next Saturday? It's her birthday."

"No." Camilla pushed the leftover gravy around her plate with her fork. They should have this party at Tally's inn. The pub there had plenty of room, and Camilla would not have to attend. Tally often treated Camilla just as rudely as Hilde did.

"You must make sure the house is clean by Friday, and we'll need some food too. You can leave work a few hours early."

Camilla opened her mouth to say no. She didn't want to ask Karin for time off for Tally's party, but Hilde swept out of the room.

"Just do it," Marit barked. "It's a couple hours." She let out a squeal and backed away, waving her finger at the corner. "There's ants over there. Get them out of here."

Camilla sighed and took care of the one ant, then returned to the kitchen to tackle the pile of dishes. She needed to stand up to her two pushy sisters, but she never would. She didn't want to risk angering Hilde, whose anger sometimes came out in a crack of her hand to Camilla's face.

Hopefully there wouldn't be many people at this party.

But she knew better. Hilde's parties were usually highly attended by the younger adults in the community. Camilla checked the stove, which was still warm, and restarted the fire to get some water boiling. She'd have to clean the ashes out too since Marit hadn't done it before making their dinner tonight.

Camilla had no desire to move to Trenten, but one thing intrigued her. Hilde had told her stories about how the people there had stoves that worked off gas instead of wood, and water that came through a conduit into the house into their sink. Nobody had to go outside to pump water from the well.

Life might be easier in Trenten than in their isolated house in the woods, but that was only if they could all get jobs.

But moving to Trenten would mean they'd have to pass over the river, and there were only two ways to cross. The first was a week's long trip way up the road to a bridge and almost another week to get to the city. They didn't have any way to carry enough supplies for such a long journey since there would be days of walking where they wouldn't see hardly anyone.

It wasn't feasible to go that way, not until they had two horses and a wagon, but the shorter way scared her even more.

The bridge that lay only fifteen minutes' walk from their home was guarded by a man-eating troll who'd taken up residence underneath the bridge hundreds of years ago, and although nobody had ever gotten a close look at him, they knew he was seven feet tall and hairy. He smelled of rotten fish and wore clothes stained with blood.

Despite the warm wash water, a shiver went up Camilla's spine.

If Marit and Hilde left, Camilla would seriously consider staying behind. She'd probably have to sell the house and find a small room to rent, but she'd rather do that than take a two-week journey to an unknown town.

She stared down at the embroidered towel her mother had made. Camilla had one just like this with her name on it, hidden away in her room so that her sisters didn't ruin it. Mother had taught her how to create the beautiful designs out of thread and needle, but she'd had little time for such extravagances now.

Her parents had not approved of Hilde and Marit moving when they were alive, but now there was nobody to discourage them from leaving.

But her sisters had been talking for years, and they would probably never actually move to Trenten. Besides, saving up enough money for two horses and a wagon would take forever.

No, no need to worry.

Chapter Two

Sunday evening, Camilla followed her sisters into town for the fall festival, all dressed in their best clothes. The festival had been her father's favorite, and for days and days before it started, he would talk it up and get Camilla as excited about it as he was.

Camilla smoothed out her skirt, which was a little more worn than Hilde and Marit's dresses. She tried to wear her clothes for as long as she could, especially since Hilde seemed to wear hers out so quickly.

"Tally!" Hilde linked arms with her best friend after she came out of her house at the edge of town, and the two chatted away.

"Is Sven coming?" Tally asked. Sven was supposedly Hilde's gentleman friend, a man she worked with, but Camilla had yet to meet him. She heard all about him though and how handsome he was.

"No, he wasn't available tonight."

"It's too bad because this festival is so pitiful. I don't even know why we're going." Hilde made a pouty face. "That reminds me, Horsten has their annual summer carnival next month, and you must come with Sven and I. There is so much to see and do."

Hilde, Tally, and Marit strolled in front of Camilla, paying her no attention, but she didn't mind. She ignored their chatter and focused on more interesting things. A small bunny ducked down at the side of the road, hoping not to be spotted. None of the three noticed the adorable thing.

They walked down the dirt road to the town center, and Camilla gazed up at the glowing lanterns hanging on all the buildings. A banjo, guitar, and harmonica played a lively tune, and several people danced in the street. Her parents would have been right there with the crowd if they'd been alive.

The sugary sweet smell of treats wafted through the air, along with the buzz of the townspeople. Hilde was wrong: their town's fall festival had much to do and see, but she was too fussy.

Camilla drifted away from her sisters, who had found their group of friends, and waded through the crowds saying hello and nodding to those she knew. She'd been saving up and couldn't wait to try some of the desserts, and she got into line at the only place she'd wanted to visit, the treat table.

"Good evening, Camilla." Sonja from the pastry shop gave her a wide smile. "How are you tonight?"

"Good, thank you." She eyed the table, trying to decide. There was too much to choose from.

"I'm thinking perhaps some krumkake for you?" Sonja winked.

"I will definitely go for the krumkake. Two, please. And a sandbakkel. It looks so delicious." She couldn't resist the yummy sandbakkel filled with custard and topped with strawberries and blueberries. She spotted the Berdahl children and told Sonja to add two more pieces of krumkake. The kids loved when Camilla made the delicate wafer-thin cookies and sometimes even helped her make them.

Sonja handed her a bag with the krumkake and then the sandbakkel. "Have you thought anymore about my offer?"

Camilla laughed. Working with Sonja would be wonderful as she was probably the only woman Camilla considered a close friend. Sonja was ten years older than Camilla, but when they got together, they had a lot of fun.

But she couldn't leave Karin and Roald and their sweet children.

"I wish I could work for you. It would be a dream, but I'd be unable to resist all those delicious sweets." Plus, Sonja wasn't able to pay as much as the Berdahls.

Sonja chuckled. "You don't eat as much of it when you're working with it all day. Trust me."

"Let me know if you ever need me to come help on Sundays though. If you're in a pinch."

"You'd be the first one I call on."

Camilla felt someone approach from behind her, so she said her goodbyes and made her way to a table to sit.

The two pieces of krumkake melted in her mouth, and she had to make sure she didn't eat the others meant for the Berdahl children. She bit into the sandbakkel and almost moaned. Sonja was the best baker in the countryside.

"Is this seat taken?"

Camilla froze, the sandbakkel poised in front of her mouth, and stared up into a set of stunning green eyes. The man's dark hair was cut shorter than how most of the men wore it around here, but he still looked good.

She realized she hadn't spoken yet and quickly licked her lips. "Uh, no... No, it is not." She pointed to the chair, her face heating. She must seem such a dunce.

"I'm Oskar." He offered his hand, and they shook as she introduced herself.

"Are you new to town, Oskar? I don't think we've met." Although she didn't know everybody in town personally, she at least knew who they were. Karin Berdahl and her ladies often had much gossip to share.

"I'm visiting my cousin, Knut Stene. Do you know him? He's trying to talk me into moving to town, and one of the things he told me to do tonight was to try Sonja's treats. Now I'm not sure what to get."

Camilla laughed. "Yes, I know Knut." He owned the general store, after all. She held the sandbakkel towards him. "I would most definitely go with the sandbakkel. The custard is so yummy. Would you like a bite?"

Her face blazed even hotter. He was a stranger, and she was offering a bite of food she'd already eaten off of.

"I'm good, thanks. But you've talked me into it."

"Camilla," Hilde said, sidling up to the table with Tally next to her. "Having *another* snack? Didn't you get enough at dinner?"

Tally took a seat, and Camilla shrunk in her chair. She pushed away the sandbakkel, the desire to finish it now gone.

"Hi, I'm Tally." She pulled her chair closer to Oskar, and Hilde plopped down in the fourth seat.

"You're Oskar, Knut's cousin, right? He was talking about you." She fluttered her long lashes at him.

"I am," Oskar chuckled, all his attention now on Tally and her big brown eyes and shiny blonde hair.

"He said you were considering moving here. You should. We have such a sad selection of shoes. The man who creates these dreadful things really needs to retire. They're functional but ugly." Tally slid her skirt up to show off her brown shoe. "Look at this hideous thing. I saw Mathilde's shoes and would love a pair or two. You do spectacular work." She finally dropped her skirt.

Camilla wanted to roll her eyes. Since their town was on the main road to Horsten, the inn was often busy with travelers, and Tally and her parents lived quite well. She even bragged about her ability to buy new shoes when Camilla and her sisters each had only one pair.

"Thank you. I need to find a new place for a store because my town does not have enough work for my mentor and myself."

"Estfold is fabulous," Hilde gushed. "The town is small, but it doesn't have that small-town claustrophobic feel like so many others."

Camilla stared at her lying sister, but she supposed Hilde wouldn't come out and tell him her real thoughts about how pathetic Estfold was. She only shared that with her family and close friends.

"Yes, we need a new shoe shop here." Tally touched Oskar's hand and smiled. "How long have you been creating your masterpieces?"

Camilla sat there and listened to the playful banter between Oskar and Tally. Why did she have to show up? It's not like Camilla thought Oskar was interested in her, but she was enjoying her conversation with him, and Tally and Hilde swooped in and took that away from her. There were a few hundred people at the festival, but somehow Hilde and Tally zeroed in on Camilla.

"I'd love to." Oskar stood, and Camilla's head whipped up. Oskar was holding his hand for Tally, and she jumped to her feet. "It was nice meeting you, Camilla. I'm sure we'll have the chance to speak again." He marched off with Tally's hand in his to where the band was playing, and a crowd was dancing.

Hilde followed behind, no goodbye to Camilla.

Oskar seemed to be a nice guy, and now he might have to make an appearance in her stories at home, one of the books with the blank pages her father had given her years ago. As a youngster, she'd used them to write stories, mostly about confident girls on fun adventures, but as she'd gotten older, those adventures tended to involve handsome and gallant men who showered their attention on the brave girl.

Oskar was interested in Tally now, but on the pages of Camilla's book, he would whisk her away from her sisters and romance her. She could even picture the illustration that would go with the story.

But that would have to wait until later.

She sighed, scanning the crowd. The Berdahl children were playing games, so now would be a good time to give them their treat. She made her way over to them and plastered a big smile on her face. If she didn't get rid of this krumkake now, she'd probably eat it herself.

Karin Berdahl stood next to Ingrid Pettersen, who Marit worked for, and Kjersti Naess. They seemed to be deep in conversation, and Camilla waited at their side for a break to ask for permission to give the children their treat.

Karin finally glanced up, her face dour. "Oh, Camilla. Hello."

"Sorry to interrupt," Camilla said demurely.

Karin waved her off. "We were discussing Isaac Berg."

"Did you hear what happened?" Kjersti asked, and Camilla shook her head. "He drank too much and went after the troll. He took his gun with him and shot it off when he came out at the bridge. The troll ran across the bridge and disappeared, and when Isaac crossed to the other side, the troll suddenly popped out again and grabbed him."

Camilla gasped. It had been a while since the troll had taken anyone. Years at least.

"That horrid creature took him before any of his friends could do a thing," Ingrid added. "It's so sad. He's left behind his wife and children." Ingrid grabbed Karin's arm. "She will need our help and support."

"I know," Karin said. "We should go see her tomorrow."

"Yes, yes. Let's do that."

Their words warmed Camilla. Karin Berdahl was a decent woman, so ready to help those in their town.

"Was there a lot of others there? Did they get a good look at him?" Camilla asked. Just thinking about it all made her queasy inside. The troll had taken so many lives. Those in town knew about him, but sometimes travelers from Horsten or Skaane would pass through, not telling anyone they were about to cross over the bridge, and the troll would grab them.

"Just some friends," Kjersti huffed. "Those men should never have gone there. They'd all been drinking."

"I don't understand why the sheriff can't catch him." Ingrid shivered and looked around the crowd for the old man charged with protecting their town.

"Years ago they tried," Kjersti said. "We were but children then, so you probably don't remember. The sheriff lost two of his men that day. One was his brother, and he's never recovered."

Ingrid sucked in a hard breath. "I didn't know that."

Camilla hadn't heard the details either, just that the sheriff was unable to catch the troll. A big sign was posted next to the bridge, but there was always those who thought it a joke and chose to ignore it.

"My father told me the story years ago." Karin dropped her gaze to the ground. "He was there too, and it haunted him until the day he died."

Her words hung heavy in the air, the noise and frivolity of the surrounding crowd unable to break through.

"I don't know how you live so close to the bridge," Ingrid said to Camilla. "I would be scared."

"He's never left the bridge," Camilla replied. In all these years, nobody has been taken unless they went on the bridge. And besides, there were others who lived even closer.

"It's so sad." Kjersti stared off across the crowd and waved to someone. "Let's not talk of this anymore. Ingrid, I want to hear about your trip to Skaane. You leave tomorrow, right?"

Before Ingrid had a chance to answer, Camilla asked Karin if her children could have the treat, and with her answer, she excused herself from the ladies.

The story of Isaac Berg weighed heavy on her mind, even as the two Berdahl children gobbled up their dessert.

No, moving to Trenten would not happen.

Chapter Three

Marit yawned, pausing at the steps of their home. This dilapidated house needed a paint job, among so many other things. It was not fair that her father died before finishing all these projects, and now they had to live in this horrid place. Nobody wanted to buy it in the state it was in, and they had no money to finish the work.

She slapped at a mosquito on her arm. Stupid bugs. Marit hated the darn forest and all its horrible insects and creatures, and she wished they lived in town. In a home like Lucas's. One without cracked windows that bugs slipped through.

Today had been such a fun day with him. In fact, the whole week had been wonderful, but he wore her out. She wanted to remove her shoes and lay down. Camilla could make dinner tonight.

She crept inside the house and up the stairs to her bedroom but stopped at the closed door to Hilde's room. She flung it open.

Marit stuck her head into the bedroom doorway and stared at Hilde lying under the blanket, back turned to the door. Her eldest sister had been sick since Monday, unable to go to school, but she'd told Marit today she was going. She was probably lazing around the house all day feeling fine and just wanted a break from her teaching job at the fancy boarding school in Horsten. As if Hilde needed a break.

Hilde might be stuck in a classroom with a group of kids, but those kids were hardly there. They went to a different room for arts or for their physical activity classes. Cripes, Hilde didn't even have to spend lunch with them. It was much different than the one-room schoolhouse in Estfold. That teacher's job, corralling children, was just like Marit's, who was responsible for the Pettersen kids all... day... long. She was the one who needed a break from keeping them and their friends busy and making lunches and entertaining them.

"What are you still doing home?" Marit asked.

Hilde rolled over and yawned, looking fine, and Marit waited for her to speak.

"After you left, I got sick again. Threw up three times today." Hilde sighed dramatically and closed her eyes. "If I go to work sick, then all the kids will get sick."

Oh please. Marit almost snorted. Hilde had such an easy job, especially with the extra perks she got from Sven.

"Can you make me some soup?" Hilde whined.

Marit wasn't the maid. That was Camilla's job. But Camilla wasn't home, and Hilde would gripe and moan if she didn't get her soup.

"Give me about half an hour." Marit turned to stalk down the hall.

"And bring it up here too," Hilde called.

Of course, Your Majesty.

Just because Hilde was the oldest didn't mean she was in charge. That idea of moving to Trenten was looking better and better every day. Marit would finally get the acclaim she deserved, and it would be so nice to work with others who would appreciate her. The head of the Estfold Theater Troop was a joke, the whole small group of awful actors was a joke, and they couldn't see talent if it hit them in the face.

But Marit and her sisters had to get past that troll on the bridge because a two-week journey by foot would never happen. Hilde said she had a spectacular idea on how to slip by the vicious creature, but she hadn't shared it yet because she didn't trust Marit. Hilde was the biggest shrew sometimes, and Marit couldn't wait to leave both her and Camilla behind in Trenten.

Hilde would never make it as an opera singer. She was so doggone lazy. Camilla could get a job because she'd take anything, but her earnings were meager, hardly enough to support the lifestyle Marit was meant to live.

Her doggone sisters were always holding her back.

Marit stoked up the fire, retrieved some water from the well, and filled a pot on the stove.

The only other bad thing about moving to Trenten was leaving Lucas. They had been intimate for a few months now, and he was so generous with his gifts.

She should talk him into coming with her because he could support her while she found her acting job. He might be reluctant to move so far away from his family though.

Marit got the vegetables out, and a movement caught her eye out the window. Camilla was back from her maid's job at the Berdahls, but instead of coming inside, she sat down on the swing under the tree. A book sat on Camilla's lap, a pencil in hand. Probably that book she was always writing in. Camilla liked to write stories about handsome men who swept her off her feet.

The stories were pure fantasy and would never happen. Camilla was the ugliest of the three sisters, and she was unpleasantly plump. Roly-poly was what Marit called her, a gross whale who refused to make herself better no matter how often Marit and Hilde tried to help her. No man would ever want her.

No, Marit didn't want to have to support Camilla in Trenten.

She sighed, setting down the long carrot, and went to the door.

"Camilla, can you come make some soup for Hilde? I started it but have other things to do."

Camilla shut her book and stood, dusting herself off. Those pathetic skirts she sewed would not fit in a place like Trenten. Marit really needed to talk to Hilde about the move. If Lucas didn't want to come along, the two of them could just go, and they'd tell Camilla they'd send for her later. They could take their horse and go the long route. It was two weeks by walking but would be much shorter by horse, and then they'd avoid the troll.

That might work.

Hilde sat at the table in the kitchen, sipping her soup, not looking one bit sick. "It's good."

"Thanks," Marit said, scooping out the last spoonful. She would miss Camilla's food when they left for Trenten, but she'd get by. She'd have a whole town of new friends and admirers. She would definitely have to find somebody to do the cleaning—that job was certainly beneath her.

A loud knock came at the door, and before any of them stood, the door swung open. A devastatingly handsome man stood in the doorway, his face red. His long blond hair was pulled tight at the nape of his neck, and he shook out his fancy blue silk shirt and ran his hands down his black trousers.

"Hilde," he huffed.

"Sven." She jumped to her feet and ran to him. "What are you doing here?"

Sven? Marit sat straighter in her chair. Hilde's gentleman friend at her school. He was better looking than Hilde had even said.

"Where have you been all week? I need the money back. They're investigating the accounts and—"

Money from what? Had he borrowed Hilde money for their journey to Trenten? Maybe it was to buy another horse and make the travel easier.

Hilde held up her hand and glared at her sisters. "I think we need to go into the other room."

Marit almost said no, but they wouldn't have listened to her, so she quickly finished her soup and left the kitchen too.

Hilde faced Sven, standing in front of the sofa as the words tumbled out of his mouth. They didn't even notice as she made her way up the stairs and went down the hallway. She opened and shut her door to make it sound like she retreated to her room, but she stood out of view from the steps instead.

"I have nothing left. Why would I? It was a gift." Hilde shot back.

"I need it back. You'll be implicated too."

"I didn't do anything. How dare you accuse me of impropriety." Hilde's voice was sharp, but Marit heard the fear behind it. This wasn't about a gift.

Marit remembered the conversation with Camilla about the missing money from Hilde's school.

"You owe me the money?" Sven yelled.

"I don't have anything," she matched his tone back.

"I'm taking Shandy," he growled.

"No," Hilde whined. "She's mine. I need her to get to work."

"Work?" Sven scoffed. "You won't have a job after this week. I won't have a job. They probably already know it was us."

Cripes, it was true. Sven must have been the one who stole from the school, and he gave it to Hilde.

"But it's not my fault." Hilde sniffed.

"But you took the money."

Marit waited as the silence lingered, and Hilde whispered quietly, "I didn't know."

"You did," he snarled.

Marit peeked around the corner in time to see Sven stomp through the door and into the kitchen. The back door slammed, and Hilde ran after him, her hands clenched. Marit tiptoed down the steps to the kitchen. Camilla stood at the sink washing dishes, staring at Hilde as she gazed out the door.

Sven stalked to the barn, flung open the door, and disappeared inside. Hilde stood there, her eyes wide. She needed to do something. He couldn't just take their horse.

Camilla turned around and mouthed, "What's going on?"

Marit shrugged. Now wasn't the time to ask Hilde. She would wait until Camilla wasn't around.

"Please don't," Hilde begged in a quiet voice as Sven led Hilde's mare to his wagon and hitched her up with the other horse, but she remained on the steps.

Sven led the horses out of the yard, and Hilde slumped against the door.

Something clicked in Marit's head, and she felt Hilde's despair flow through her. They were losing their horse. They had planned on selling Shandy to get money for their trip and for lodging once they arrived in Trenten.

"Why did he take our horse?" Camilla asked tentatively.

Hilde stared at her, her lip curled into a sneer, but didn't answer. Then she stomped away.

This couldn't be happening. They wouldn't have any money now for the move.

"What did you do?" Marit squealed and chased after her up the stairs.

Hilde ignored her until they reached her room. She spun around, her tight face red. "I didn't do anything. Sven gave me gifts just like you get from Lucas."

"That's different. Lucas has his own money. He didn't steal it from his employer."

"I didn't know he was stealing it."

Marit pointed her finger at her sister. "You liar. He said you knew. I heard him. And now you're out of a job, and we've lost our horse. How are we going to get to Trenten now?"

"I... I..." Hilde flung her hands up in the air. "I don't know." Some of the anger fell off her face as if she suddenly realized the consequences. "I'll find another job here."

"There's no teaching job in Estfold."

"Then Skaane. I can go there." Hilde sunk onto her bed.

Sometimes Hilde was as dumb as Camilla.

"You can't walk to Skaane. Do I need to remind you that he took Shandy?" Marit huffed. "And besides, when they hear what you did, they won't even consider you. What if Sven turns around and blames you? You aren't there to defend yourself."

Marit felt like the big sister suddenly. Hilde had gone and done something foolish, and they were all paying for it, and now Marit had to step in and tell her how things would be.

"This is what will happen," Marit said. "You will probably have to find a job cleaning. And we will have to save up all our money until we have enough." Marit clenched her hands. This meant she would have to do the same. No more spending the money Lucas gave her on frivolous things. Her dreadful life was about to get worse.

"It'll only be eight months, I bet. Maybe nine. It won't be so bad. Just a touch longer." Hilde acted like it was no big deal, but it was. They hadn't really shared their plan with Camilla yet, but they had decided to go.

Now was definitely the time to invite Lucas along. And even if he said no, he'd give her the money for a new horse. He had plenty in the bank after all.

Marit glared at her sister. This was Hilde's fault. She'd let Sven talk her into foolish things just because he had a devilishly handsome face.

"We'd better cancel Tally's party."

"No. She's depending on me. Everybody is. We can't cancel now," Hilde whined. "Besides, somebody will have a lead on a job."

"But it'll be too much money. We need that money." Every bit.

"We'll just have less food and drink, and I'll have some of the boys spread the word that we need some help. That's no big deal."

Marit sighed. This whole situation was horrible, but Lucas would help her out. She would talk to him as soon as possible.

Doggone Hilde. She was so dumb sometimes.

Chapter Four

Camilla surveyed the full counter, all the food she had prepared for Tally's birthday, including sugary treats and other dishes.

Hilde picked up the bowl of unpeeled hardboiled eggs. "Why isn't this done?"

The chopped ham filling was already made, but Camilla still needed to peel the eggs so she could stuff them. If only Hilde and Marit had helped her out more.

"I'm sorry. Karin only let me off at noon. I haven't had enough time. If you two had started things before I got home, I wouldn't be behind."

"Don't look at me," Marit sniped. "I was busy at the Pettersen's all week." She slipped out of the kitchen, still unwilling to help.

Hilde glowered. "You know my food won't be anywhere near as wonderful as yours. Nobody would ever come back here again."

She could at least help with some of the simple things, but no, Hilde had spent the afternoon with Tally gossiping and drinking akevitt. In fact, Hilde had hardly done a thing all this past week since Sven had shown up and taken their horse. She hadn't looked much for jobs and had lazed around the house.

From the conversations Camilla eavesdropped on, she had put things together. Her sister was a thief, sort of. She might not have taken the money herself, but she was well aware that Sven was giving her stolen money.

Camilla hoped the gossip from Horsten wouldn't make it down to Estfold. Hilde needed to find another job.

"Where's my kransekake? Is it ready?" Tally strutted into the room, her long blonde hair swishing behind her. She wore a brand-new dress and bright shiny shoes. Tally spotted the tower cake and ran a finger through the white icing. "It was supposed to be eight layers."

"I'm sorry." Camilla bowed her head. "I didn't have time." The cake had only four of the concentric rings stacked up.

"Camilla." Hilde's hands flung to her hips. "She wanted eight. She's twenty-eight now. The least you could've done is gotten this right. She's our best friend."

She wasn't Camilla's best friend.

"This thing is tiny," Tally whined.

"I'm sorry. I didn't have enough time."

Tally huffed and stabbed a meatball from the bowl, took a bite, and stepped over to the akevitt on the counter and refilled her glass

"You'd better get working faster," Hilde commanded. "There's only two hours left, and you still need to finish cleaning up." She glanced down at the dirty bowls but didn't offer to wash them.

A horse galloped into the yard, and Camilla stared out the window. What was Ingrid Pettersen doing here? She was supposed to be out of town.

Ingrid slid off her horse, straightened her skirt, and patted her hands over her hair, and stalked up to the porch.

Camilla was about to call Marit, but Ingrid screamed Marit's name.

Ingrid stood on the porch, her eyes flaring. "Marit, you get down here right now." She stomped her foot so hard she winced, but the angry look stayed on her face.

"What's wrong?" Hilde said through the open door as Tally looked on in curiosity. Camilla stayed back in the room.

"You tell your lying sister to come here. Now!" She pointed an angry finger at Hilde and narrowed her eyes even farther.

"Go get Marit," Hilde directed, and Camilla rushed off. Marit was coming down the stairs.

"Mrs. Pettersen is here," Camilla whispered.

"I heard," Marit scoffed. "I'm not deaf."

She headed out to the porch and to the steps, and Camilla, Hilde, and Tally followed behind but stood back.

"Did you really think I wouldn't find out about how you played house with my husband while the children and I were gone?" Ingrid snarled. "You are done in this town, you strumpet. You will never work here again."

Marit's upper lip curled into a sneer, and she stood tall. "It's not my fault you can't satisfy your husband."

Camilla gasped, covering her mouth with her hands. This couldn't be true. Marit couldn't be having relations with Lucas Pettersen. He was her employer, and he was married… with children.

Marit was known to have relations with single men sometimes but never a married one.

"You may have bedded him, but you are nothing to him. He doesn't love you. He doesn't even want you. You took advantage of him, but you will no longer."

Marit rolled her eyes. "You shouldn't have gotten old and ugly."

"Marit," Camilla whispered, barely able to believe her sister. The appalling words were not even true. Camilla didn't know Ingrid well, but she was beautiful, and the ladies in Karin Berdahl's circle said Ingrid was kind and generous.

Marit pointed her finger right back at Ingrid. "You've been mistreating him for years, and now he's found a real woman."

"You?" Ingrid gave a harsh laugh. "Do you really believe he will leave his children for you? Do you think he will give up my money to be with you?"

"It's not your money. It's his." Marit smirked, and Camilla wanted to wipe the arrogant look off her sister's face.

"Foolish girl. You believed his lies. He has no money. It belongs to my parents, and if I chose to throw him out of the house, he would have nothing."

Marit's face clouded over, and her lips twitched, but she folded her arms and straightened herself.

"I don't care," she spit and dashed into the house.

Ingrid focused her outrage on Hilde. "The both of you are disgusting. Ruining lives without another thought. We all know what happened at your school and that you're a thief."

Hilde threw up her hands and sputtered. "I didn't do anything."

"Of course you didn't." She said the words slowly, like she didn't actually mean them.

Ingrid was right. Camilla's sisters were disgusting. Stealing money and husbands.

"I need not stand here and take this." Hilde spun around and stomped into the house, Tally following.

Camilla was left alone with the furious woman. She had no desire to defend her sisters, no doubt that what Ingrid claimed was true.

"I'm sorry." Camilla's head fell. Her family held no honor anymore

"You are not your sisters," Ingrid said gruffly, but her face softened. "Your parents would be so disappointed in how they have turned out, but I know you will not take the same paths they have chosen."

Ingrid hastened to her horse and galloped out of their yard, and Camilla watched her retreating figure.

It hit her then. Marit had lost her job, and with the way the Pettersens were loved and admired in town, nobody else would hire her.

And Ingrid had known about Hilde's misdeeds, and she would pass that information on to her sister in Skaane. Neither Hilde nor Marit would get a job there either.

Horsten and Skaane were the only other towns near enough with jobs. The next closest towns were several weeks' journey by foot since they had no horses.

That meant Camilla was the only one earning any money. They'd never have enough for the bills that their parents had left behind plus everything else.

She rubbed her throbbing temples, not knowing what would happen after this.

Inside, the three women sat talking about. Camilla stayed back, and they didn't even notice her.

"Jonas Strand's wife is sick," Tally said. "Doctor Vinter doesn't expect her to make it more than a couple months."

Oh no, Camilla hadn't heard that news. The poor woman.

"Jonas Strand is hideous," Hilde sniped. "I would have to be desperate to bed him."

"But his family is wealthy," Tally said.

"I'd consider it," Marit giggled. "I'll just close my eyes."

Camilla hid her gasp. Jonas Strand's wife would soon be gone, and their family would be devastated.

"Finn Holgersen might be an option." Tally shrugged. "I've heard he's invited Nora Naess into his bed, and you two are both better than her. I noticed the new dress she was wearing the other day. She didn't buy that from working in the general store."

Marit and Hilde both nodded in agreement.

What is wrong with you? Camilla wanted to scream. Finn Holgersen was yet another married man with a family. All her sisters cared about was taking advantage of men, using them, and not caring if they tore a family apart.

Her sisters were truly disgusting. Camilla stomped up to them. "Did you really bed Lucas Pettersen?"

"He seduced me," Marit growled. "He told me how beautiful I was. How special I was."

Marit had made it sound like she'd been working hard all week, that she was caring for the Pettersen children while their mother was gone, but it was all lies.

She'd even come home with that new dress, which was probably Ingrid's.

"We need to postpone the party," Camilla said. She was now the only person making money, and until the sisters got jobs, things would be tight. And it would be difficult to get jobs around here.

"Don't be a dunce, Camilla," Hilde said. "Everybody will be here soon. We've already made the food. What are we going to do? Let it go to waste?"

"But there's drinks and other things that wouldn't be wasted. We can sell the akevitt."

Marit gave a dramatic sigh. "Why would you do that to Tally? She's been looking forward to this for the last month."

Tally nodded her head along. "Things have been tough lately."

Tough? Things were never tough for Tally, not the way her parents took care of her. Camilla's sisters would never listen to her though, no matter how hard she tried. They didn't even realize the consequences of their actions, the people that they hurt.

And their money would be gone soon.

"Don't you have things to do still?" Hilde folded her arms and glared at Camilla. "There's not much time left."

"Sorry. I'll be done on time." Camilla spun around and headed back to the kitchen.

Camilla mostly stayed in the kitchen at first, which meant a lot of time to think about what her sisters had done and what could happen to them.

If Ingrid Pettersen was angry enough, she could keep people in town from selling goods to Camilla's family. Hopefully, Ingrid wouldn't go that far.

Night had fallen, and she only had one lamp in the dark kitchen, so she retreated to the brightly lit parlor. A quick headcount showed almost twenty people. She put on a smile and approached one of the friendlier women in the room.

Hanne returned the smile. "There she is. Camilla, do you know Elin?" She linked her arms through the other woman's. "She is down from Horsten visiting. Her sister is married to Roy."

"It's a pleasure to meet you. I haven't seen Roy in a while." Tally's oldest brother was much nicer than his baby sister.

"I thought it was a favorable time for a visit. My husband's school is going through a little turmoil, and I brought the kids down to get away. They're only three and four, so they're not in school yet."

"What's going on?" Hanne asked.

Camilla didn't move. Elin had to be talking about Hilde's school. Hanne had been more of Marit's friend, so maybe she didn't know Hilde had been teaching there.

"It's a shame. The headmaster has been stealing money from the school. The day before I left, he was arrested."

Camilla gathered the folds of her skirt in her hands. Were they coming after Hilde too? Would she be arrested? Camilla steadied her voice. "Was anyone else implicated or just the headmaster?"

"I don't know." Elin shrugged. "I didn't have much information."

47

"That's so sad. I hope he goes to jail." Hanne shook her head. "On a brighter note, remember those meatballs you were raving about earlier. Camilla is the one who made them."

"You did? Oh, they were delicious." Elin gave Camilla's arm a squeeze and raved about them. It was nice to feel appreciated for a change.

She spoke with Elin and Hanne for a bit and eventually made her way over to Oskar.

"So have you decided to move to Estfold?" she asked him.

"I did." He smiled warmly. "I will be returning to Reissin next week so I can move everything with my wagon."

She should ask if she could send Marit and Hilde with him to live in Reissin, but that wouldn't work.

All three would have to leave. Camilla couldn't pay for the bills alone, and her sisters would never send money back to her.

But it's not like he had the ability to bring three women back on his one horse anyway. Maybe the people who claimed the towns other than Horsten and Skaane were more than a week's walk away were wrong.

"How far away is Reissin? If you were walking, I mean."

Oskar gave her a funny look. "I don't know exactly. I've never met anybody crazy enough to walk the road, but I'd guess eight or nine days."

Camilla sighed. With all that walking, they'd need to bring extra pairs of shoes, and they could not afford extra shoes right now.

"Oskar," Tally called, slithering up to him. "Didn't I tell you to meet me out back?"

He grimaced. "I was about to leave and then started speaking with Camilla. Sorry."

Ha. Camilla distracted a man from Tally. She let her satisfaction show on her face, but Tally's angry glare drained that away.

Tally slipped her smile back on and turned to Oskar, looping her arm through his. "Let's go. I want to show you the swing."

He excused himself, and they went through the kitchen door. Camilla waited a moment and followed behind. She wanted a drink and then would retreat to her room upstairs.

The kitchen was dark since Tally had taken the oil lamp with her, and Camilla stood there watching the two. Oskar accompanied Tally to the swing hanging from one of the giant oaks and held it still while she sat.

Noise drifted through the walls from the party in the next room, and Camilla stared out the window.

Tally and Oskar sat hand-in-hand on the swing as the crickets and frogs and other creatures of the night serenaded them.

Camilla clenched the washrag from the sink in her hands. Oskar was an honest man, and he deserved a woman who would be true to him, a woman more like Camilla. And perhaps if Tally had not come along at the festival and stolen Oskar away, Camilla might be out on the swing with him. Perhaps they would be starting a relationship that would lead to Camilla escaping life with these two shameful sisters.

Light spilled into the room from the parlor.

"What are you doing?" Marit demanded from the doorway, her hand on her hip. She ambled over, her body swaying, and the door closed, enveloping the two sisters in darkness.

"Nothing."

Marit stared at the window and let out a guffaw, her breath smelling of akevitt. "Are you spying on Tally and Oskar?"

"No. I was only standing in the quiet room." Her excuse was pathetic, but she had no others ready. She glanced out the window at Oskar. She and he might not have been destined to be together, but just once she wanted a chance at happiness too. She thought of the story she'd created in her journal of her and Oskar, and heat filled her cheeks. Good thing Marit couldn't see her face in the dark.

"Are you jealous?" Marit's voice rose high on the last word, and she poked Camilla in the side. "Jealous. Jealous." Marit's laugh turned dark. "Do you really think he'd go for someone like you? He obviously likes intelligent women."

Camilla bit back the tears. Marit was such a witch sometimes.

"At least I didn't bed my boss," she sniped.

"Well, I bedded your boss." Marit cackled, and Camilla froze, her mind spinning.

"You've been with Roald Berdahl?"

Marit couldn't have sunk so low to put Camilla's job at risk.

"Not him," Marit sneered. "William Raabe. And only twice," Marit slurred. "He wasn't that good. I don't want to see him again, but he keeps bugging me."

Camilla wanted to melt into the floor even though she and Marit were the only ones in the room. William was Karin's brother, who she'd worked for a short time before going to Karin and Roald's.

And William was just as married as Lucas Pettersen.

"Have you slept with every married man in town?" This story just got worse and worse all the time. Marit had always been a little loose, but bedding married men a whole new level.

"Of course not," Marit scoffed. "Most married men won't give me a second glance."

Probably because they knew her reputation. Camilla thought back to a few years ago when Ivar Falk had seemed interested in her, but after a month, he'd stopped calling on her, and she hadn't known why. It had been after the time she'd run into him in town when he was talking to Marit.

Had he... had they... Marit had known then he was calling on Camilla.

Camilla steeled herself. "Did you bed Ivar Falk?"

"No." She sighed. "He was so handsome, but he refused me though, the silly boy."

"Was this during or after he had been calling on me?" The pit in Camilla's stomach grew.

"After," she scoffed, but Camilla heard the lie in her voice. Marit had chased after a man Camilla was interested in, and not long after, he walked away.

Had he thought she was loose like Marit? Had he not wanted such a woman for a wife? Or maybe he hadn't wanted a sister-in-law like Marit.

Sofie, the woman he married a year later was a sweet and wonderful woman, and she had tried to be happy for them, but she never understood why he broke things off.

Now she knew.

Camilla needed air, but she couldn't go outside, so she slipped through the party and up to her room. She wanted to get lost in her fantasies, her book of honorable men and romance.

In her bedroom, Camilla dug out her special book of stories. The left pages held the sketches, and on the right were the written words. Camilla wasn't the best writer, but her drawings were pretty decent.

Her pencil moved easily across the paper, creating a large oak tree and a swing, the moon shining down on the setting. She drew two bodies embracing in a kiss. The blue eyes of the woman were not visible, but her brown hair barely touched her shoulders, just like Camilla's.

As soon as she finished the drawing, Camilla started on the story.

Oskar led Camilla out of the boring party to the swing under the grand oak tree. The quiet moon gazed down, and fireflies flew around them.

"Camilla, you are so beautiful. I'm tired of being around all these silly women, and I'm so glad to sit here with you on this swing," Oskar said.

"Thank you for inviting me out here. I've been waiting for a chance for us to talk again."

This is how life would be with an honorable man, but she'd also have to keep her sisters away.

But if he was an honorable man, she wouldn't have to worry.

She gazed out the window at the full moon looking down upon her. According to Marit, there were honorable men out there, and one day Camilla would find a man who loved her and wanted to take care of her.

A loud cackle sounded behind her, and someone ripped her book out of her hands. Tally smirked down at the pages, a laugh building in her eyes.

"Heavens, Marit said you were jealous, but this is absurd."

"Give it back." Camilla jumped out of bed and tried to grab the book, but Tally swung it away. "You can't possibly imagine that Oskar would be interested in you. Not when he has a woman like me." Tally laughed again and dashed out of the door. Camilla sprinted behind her, but Tally was too fast, already reaching the steps and racing downstairs.

"Lordy, Oskar! Look at this," Tally screeched. She gripped the book with a smirk on her face, and Oskar peered over her shoulder reading along with her. "She's writing about you. She seems to fancy you." Tally laughed and finally looked up.

Oh no. Oskar was reading her silly fantasy, a confused look on his face. He finally drew his gaze to Camilla's, and he smiled softly. "You are very talented, Camilla. You really drew those pictures?"

She nodded without answering.

"I have a mother who is not happy to hear I'm moving to Estfold. Would you consider doing a portrait that I can present her when I return home?"

"Ahhh…" She couldn't get the words out. He couldn't seriously be asking her to draw his picture.

"I'm sorry. I don't suppose that would leave you much time. Is it even possible?"

Camilla's muddled head would barely let through a thought. "Yes, I'm sure I could."

Tally stared at them in disbelief, and Camilla tried her best to ignore her.

"I will pay you for it too," he assured her.

"That's not necessary. I would love to." Someone actually wanted to possess her work. She could barely hide her smile, but then she caught sight of Tally's dark face.

"She would love to provide you services," Tally mimicked Camilla's voice, waving the book around.

"Give me my book back." Camilla stuck out her trembling arm, but Tally slapped it away.

"What's going on?" someone said at the same time Oskar called Tally's name sternly.

"Attention, everyone." Tally clapped her hands loudly, backing away from Camilla and Oskar, and the room grew silent.

"We have a storyteller in our midst." Tally started reading off the page about the love story of Camilla and Oskar that ended in a kiss. A few gasps and chuckles came from the group.

"Tally, quit it," Oscar said, stepping towards her.

"What is that?" Hilde stomped over and ripped the book out of Tally's hands.

"It appears your sister is in love with Oskar." Tally smirked, ignoring Oskar's angry face.

"Heavens, you did this?" Hilde laughed. "Look at this." She flipped back a few pages and read, several others crowding in around her.

Hilde's head swung up, and she scanned the room. "Ludvig, there's a story about you too. Apparently, you took my sister to a dance." She held up the book to display the picture of Ludvig and Camilla dancing under the stars.

Oh no. Please no.

Camilla wanted to disappear. She hadn't desired after Ludvig because he had been interested in Hilde for a time, but he'd ended up on the pages of her book because he'd always treated her well.

Ludvig glanced at her from across the room, looking so confused. He was a decent man, and now he'd been shamed too. He'd never shown any interest in Camilla but had always been nice to her.

Some of the others crowded around the girls, and the buzz filled the parlor again.

Marit butted her way over and joined in to partake in the fun. "You need to work on your drawings." She laughed and then sucked in a hard breath. "Ronny Aamot. Really, Camilla?"

Ronny Aamot wasn't the most handsome man around, but he was a hard worker and a gentleman.

They were only stories, written to help her escape the drudgery of her life, never meant to be seen by anyone, and now her sisters were sharing her private thoughts with everyone.

Camilla's face burned as hot as an oven. She would never live this down.

She spun around to escape. Oskar leaned against the wall, his face pale. She stopped, and he looked down at her.

"I'm sorry. I didn't mean to embarrass you." She hung her head.

"There's nothing to be sorry for," he gruffed. "Tally was wrong to—"

"Oskar?" Tally called.

Camilla rushed past Oskar, passed through the kitchen, and slipped out the door to the backyard. She ran into the trees and slumped down behind one of the oaks, the bark scratching her back.

Marit and Hilde would share the whole book with their guests, and everybody would laugh at her silly stories and amateur drawings and the idea that these men wanted her. She shouldn't have taken out the book to work on it and just should've stayed downstairs.

The move to Trenten seemed like it might happen. Her sisters wouldn't be able to get jobs anywhere, and she'd be the laughing stock in town. They would have to brave the troll, escape off to a new town, and she would have to get away from her sisters—the awful women they were.

Ingrid Pettersen was right.

Her parents would be horrified to see how things had turned out.

Chapter Five

Marit hiked through the trees back to her house the next morning. She'd left early to find Lucas, knowing his witch-of-a-wife and children would be at church while he stayed home.

She opened her clenched hand and smacked a branch that was in her way. He had the gall to yell at her to leave his house, had told her *she* ruined his marriage. Words so different from the ones he'd whispered to her in bed.

She should have never considered inviting him to Trenten. He was an awful man, and she never wanted to see him again.

Marit and her sisters needed to get out of town, and they couldn't wait for Camilla to earn money for another horse. Ingrid Pettersen would keep Marit from getting another job in town, and Hilde had little chance too.

It was all Lucas Pettersen's fault. Marit deserved a man who would treat her better, and she'd find plenty of those men once she moved. But in Trenten, she wouldn't have to depend on a man.

No, she wasn't giving up men, but they would be there to serve her after she made a name for herself. They would grovel at her feet and want to please her.

Hilde said she'd share her plan today, and Marit couldn't wait to hear it. Hopefully it involved leaving Camilla behind.

At least the party last night had been a success, and in a weird way, it was due to Camilla and her stories. The girl had a wild imagination and yet was so boring. Never once did her stories involve a bed, and they mostly featured passionate kisses on the swing or behind the barn. The most daring drawing was a shirtless Ronny Aamot, whose body was drawn much more generously than real life.

Marit rushed up the steps into the parlor, hoping Camilla was done cleaning.

"How could you be so dim?" Hilde slapped Camilla in the back of the head. Cripes, Marit had almost missed the show.

"You humiliated Tally. And poor Oskar." Hilde crossed her arms and glared at Camilla as she cowered on the sofa. Marit hadn't thought Oskar had been embarrassed, but she wasn't about to interrupt Hilde's tongue lashing.

"Tally really liked Oskar, and he was so ashamed, he left the party. Tally was devastated that he wouldn't speak to her."

Once again, Hilde was slightly off. Oskar had sent Tally several disgusted looks before he excused himself and left. Tally, nor Hilde, would ever admit that it was Tally's actions that caused him to leave.

"Hilde, you really can't blame her," Marit said. Her two sisters looked up, Camilla with hope in her eyes. "I mean, what else do you expect her to do? Only the men of her fantasies will be with her."

Camilla's head dropped again, and Hilde smirked. "It's about time you got here. We need to talk to Camilla about what we discussed last night."

They hadn't spoken last night about anything, not that Marit recalled. Hilde had drunk too much akevitt, but Marit had been clearheaded at the end of the night. Well, not quite clearheaded, but she remembered most of the party.

"Go ahead," Marit said.

"We decided last night to leave for Trenten on Tuesday or Wednesday."

Camilla gasped. "But we have no horses, and we can't carry two weeks' worth of supplies."

"Not to mention, we can't carry enough food." Marit stared at her crazy older sister. They couldn't walk, and there were several stretches where they wouldn't see anybody for days.

Marit slapped her mouth shut; she was supposedly in on the plan. She scoured her memory for something… anything Hilde might have said last night, but she came up with nothing.

Hilde smiled triumphantly. "We will cross the troll bridge."

"No." Camilla covered her mouth. "The troll just got Isaac Berg recently. It's probably awakened his taste for blood again."

There's no way Marit would take the chance on becoming a troll's dinner.

"I have a plan. Why don't you sit down." Hilde motioned to the sofa, and Marit took a seat next to Camilla.

"So I will be the first one to cross the road," Hilde continued. "I will tell the troll that I am the first of four sisters, and that our fourth sister has volunteered to go with him and be his meal."

"But there's only three of us." Camilla gathered her skirt in her hands and twisted the faded fabric.

"Marit goes next," Hilde said, pointing to her middle sister. "She'll say the same thing. And then, Camilla, you go after that. You tell him that your last sister is coming, and he'll let you go. He won't know there's not a fourth sister until we're all safely on the other side."

Camilla shook her head. "But he might not believe us."

"Of course he would." Marit was a spectacular actress after all. This plan of Hilde's might work.

But that meant Camilla would make it across the bridge too. Trenten would be so much better if her little sister was not there. Why did Hilde want to bring her along? Maybe just she and Hilde should try her plan alone but claim they had a third sister. Camilla had her decent job with the Berdahls and could stay.

Hilde rolled her eyes. "Marit is right. And to help our story, Tally has volunteered to stand at the edge of the bridge with us, and we will say she is the fourth sister."

"And she'll be safe as long as she doesn't step onto the bridge," Marit added. Hilde was a genius. It wouldn't be long, and they'd be on the road to Trenten and their new lives.

"Tally has agreed to this?" Camilla asked.

"Yes," Hilde sniped. "Didn't you hear what I said?"

Camilla dropped her skirt and stared at her feet. She was not the smartest girl around.

"What will happen to the house and all our things?" Camilla asked.

"It's not our house anyway," Hilde said. "It will go back to the bank. And I don't know what they'll do with our stuff. We'll have no need for it anymore though."

Camilla looked around the room like she'd miss the place, the awful house with its cool drafts and worn floors and old furniture. The least their parents could have done was left them a decent house to sell.

They discussed the plan more, and Camilla finally left.

"Why do we have to bring her along?" Marit whined, after making sure Camilla was out of the room.

Hilde grinned. "That's the wonderful part. We won't. We'll both tell the troll that he can have the two sisters. Tally and Camilla. He'll be even more likely to let us pass with two meals."

"But you can't let him take Tally." Marit gave her sister a dazed look. Hilde couldn't give up her best friend to a troll.

Hilde smacked Marit in the head. "Dum dum. Tally won't come down. Only Camilla will. And we'll be on the other side by then."

"But…" That meant… "The troll will kill her."

"No, he won't. He won't want her anyway. She's big and fat and ugly, and he'll let her go. I'm not really sure those stories are true anyway."

"But didn't you hear what Camilla said about Isaac Berg?"

"Marit." Hilde sighed and sat next to Marit on the sofa. "Most likely, the troll won't get her, but even if he does, think about it. Whose life has the least potential out of all of us?"

No question there. Camilla had no talents and at best would only get a job cleaning at an inn or something worse. Camilla's life would be no better than it was here. Working and cleaning and taking care of others.

Hilde's voice grew serious. "Camilla would probably be proud to give up her life for her older sisters. You've heard her say how she misses Mother and Father."

It was true.

"Our parents would be proud of her sacrifice, and we would be grateful too." Hilde laid her hand on Marit's arm and grinned. "Think about it. We can find a lovely boarding house in Trenten. Things will be so much cheaper if it's just the two of us."

"We would only need one bed," Marit added. She hadn't shared a bed with Camilla since their parents died, and she didn't look forward to sharing with Hilde.

"We say that the last sister is the most beautiful of all, and the troll will let us cross. We'll make sure that our hair is a mess and wear some tattered clothes." Hilde glanced towards the steps. "Maybe we'll need to wear Camilla's clothes."

"I still think a troll might want someone plump like her."

"Yes, he might," Hilde finally agreed. "So we'll just have to use our beauty to charm him. It shouldn't be hard. Trolls are notoriously dumb."

"They are?" Marit hadn't heard that before.

"The next step is to get our bags packed," Hilde said. "I wish we had a horse and wagon so we could haul our trunks, but now we'll be limited to whatever we can put in our pack. And we really should leave by Tuesday."

"Sounds like a plan." Marit smiled. She quickly made a list in her head of the things she would put in her pack. Thankfully the walk on the other side of the bridge would not be far.

In less than a year, Marit would be a star, and when she returned back to Estfold, everybody would bow at her feet.

Chapter Six

Marit stomped up the steps of her house, her sack hanging from her arm. She tried to wipe her muddy shoes on the rug, but it wouldn't come off.

Stupid forest. Stupid town.

It was such a good thing they were leaving because the people in this town were so disrespectful. She slammed the door, and Hilde jumped. She took in Marit's red face and smirked. "What's wrong?"

Marit tossed the sack to the floor and then regretted it. She might have bruised the apples inside. Oh well.

"It's the close-minded people in town. That's what's wrong. I was at the general store, and Mathilde refused to serve me. Knut came over and pushed her away so I could purchase my apples and jerky. She's such a shrew."

Hilde laughed. "She's friends with Ingrid."

"But I never did anything to Mathilde." Marit huffed. Mathilde was jealous and probably thought Knut might be interested in Marit too.

Hilde laughed even harder, and Marit glared at her. She was glad to be getting out of here if that's how the townspeople would treat her. She studied Hilde.

"Why are we leaving so quickly?" They could have let Camilla earn a bit more money before they left, but Hilde had wanted to go so soon.

She thought back to the party and how someone had said Sven was arrested.

Marit gasped. "Are they coming for you? Are they arresting you along with Sven?"

"I didn't do anything," Hilde sputtered. "I figured we might as well get out of here."

Hilde stomped away to gather her things. She was lying too. She had spent the money Sven gave her, and the sheriff in Horsten would probably be out here soon to retrieve it, and when she couldn't give it back, Hilde would be arrested too.

This was all Hilde's fault.

Marit slipped up to her tiny room and stared at the crack in her bedroom window.

Good riddance to this house. Not only was it in horrible shape, but it had grown too crowded over the past two years, and it would be a relief to only deal with Hilde.

Once Marit was discovered, she'd leave Hilde behind and move into the life she deserved.

She strapped on her walking shoes and packed all her best clothes into the pack. Thankfully Lucas had presented her with a beautiful dress from Horsten before he'd abandoned her. She would think of that dolt every time she wore the dress. He'd made a big mistake treating her like he did

The only bad part about this journey would be her sore feet. At least it was only a few hours' walk and not two weeks.

"All ready?" Tally said somberly. Marit would miss her too, but they'd find new friends.

"You sure you don't want to go with?" Hilde asked.

Marit rolled her eyes. Tally wouldn't do very well in Trenten either. She worked the kitchen at her parents' inn, but she couldn't do much more than cook, and her food was only slightly better than decent. She'd drag Marit and Hilde down, and they'd have to pay to help support her too.

"No. One day I'll come to Trenten. We'll have a grand old time."

Marit almost snorted. Tally would never make the trip to visit them, but perhaps when Marit and Hilde were rich, they could send for her.

Camilla stared up at the house before they left but didn't say anything. This house was nothing but a trash heap, nothing to be attached to. Marit sure wouldn't miss it or this dumb town.

They walked for a short distance through the forest path until they reached the bend in the road right before the bridge.

"All right, this is the plan," Hilde said. "We'll all gather at the edge so the troll can see us. I'll go first and explain that our last sister is willing to sacrifice herself, and he'll let me pass. Then Marit will go, and as soon as Camilla makes it across, Tally will take off."

Everybody nodded in agreement. Marit's stomach twisted in knots. At least Hilde offered to go first. If the troll grabbed her and dragged her away, Marit could run off herself.

Hilde's gaze lingered on Marit for a few moments. Hilde wouldn't offer both sisters, would she? No, Hilde needed Marit. They'd have more money between the two of them.

"See you on the other side." Marit grinned, hoping Hilde would return it. She did, and Marit relaxed a little. Hilde and Tally hugged, Tally giving them well wishes and safe travels, and they all walked around the bend.

The stone bridge lay before them, long and narrow, until it disappeared into the trees on the far side.

They stood there in silence, each lost in their own thoughts. Hilde made no move towards the path, and the seconds turned into minutes until finally Marit nudged her. Hilde seemed to be forcing her smile as she waved to them all, but she went off the road onto the path.

She took a confident step onto the bridge. A large figure popped out of nowhere. Camilla grabbed Marit's arm, and for once Marit let her keep it there. If the troll took Hilde, they'd have to figure out another plan, and Marit had no clue what they would do.

This had to work.

The troll was taller than Hilde, wearing brown clothes. One minute passed. Then two. Hilde's hand swung around as she spoke to the troll, and he glanced their way. They weren't close enough to see the details of his face, but his hair was thick and bushy, and his gaze burned into Marit.

He frowned and turned back to Hilde, and he almost seemed to be arguing with her, pointing down the bank to the river. Hilde shook her head violently. Marit took deep breaths to steady her heart. *This has to work.*

They remained there, talking such a long time until finally Hilde stepped away from the troll, and he disappeared down the side of the bridge. Hilde marched across the span, and Marit held her breath, waiting for the troll to return.

Soon Hilde reached the middle, turned with a big smile on her face, and gave her sisters a thumbs up.

This would work.

Hilde kept walking. She was almost there, almost to the end.

It was Marit's turn, and she looked at Camilla. "See you on the other side."

Good riddance, she thought. One less worry for Marit to have in Trenten.

Hilde was now out of sight. Marit should have never doubted her oldest sister.

Some of her original nerves remained, and her palms sweated heavily along with her forehead. But Hilde had passed, so Marit would too.

She proceeded to the edge of the bridge and stopped.

Go back. The words flew threw her head, but she ignored them. Hilde would be annoyed if she took too long. Freedom and a new life were so close, and she could almost taste it.

Marit took a step onto the bridge. She took two steps, then three. The scent of putrid garbage filled her nose as the troll towered over her. Moth-ridden clothes with stains covered his body, and his wild bushy hair hadn't seen a comb nor wash in years.

"Stop," he said, his voice gruff, his rancid breath flowing over her. A chill spread up Marit's back.

He won't eat me, she repeated to herself several times and stayed rooted to the bridge.

"I need you to listen to me," he continued. "You—"

"I have another sister behind me. She's probably a full meal for your whole family." Did trolls even have families? Did they have kids? This one was ugly as a wild boar with his crooked nose and his large forehead. The females were probably just as nasty.

"Wait, what—"

"I'm making the same deal with you. You let my first sister go, and now if you let me go, you'll get the third sister. She's way bigger than me, and if I don't continue across the bridge, she'll turn around and go home. And you can't give up a meal like that."

Marit pointed to Camilla and Tally still standing on the road. Tally would have left earlier except Camilla needed to think she was part of the plan, the fourth sister.

"She's up there. See her?"

The troll stared at Marit. God, she hoped he preferred chubby girls over beautiful girls. She breathed out of her mouth so she didn't have to smell his disgusting stank. Maybe she should have said he could have Tally too. She was pretty after all, and Tally wouldn't come down anyway.

The troll crossed his arms, studying her like a bug. "So, what you're telling me is…" He paused and rubbed his chin. "That if I grant you passage, you will let me have your third sister." He glanced down to the other end of the bridge and back to Marit. "Why would you do that?"

"Look." Marit waved to the trees. "You can see her. She doesn't have a happy life. She's miserable all the time, and she wants to help her sisters by sacrificing herself. I swear though, she's huge. Enough food for a week. I mean, I don't know how much you eat, but she'd feed you for a while."

Marit eyed him curiously. The troll was definitely disgusting and all, but she'd expected him to be nastier. Mean and rotten.

"But that's not what your sister said."

Doggone Hilde. Did she break from the plan?

"And what did she say?"

"That your youngest sister likes to hit the both of you. She said you are trying to escape the violence of your home. I tried—"

"Well, that's true too," Marit huffed. Hilde should have shared this story with Marit so she didn't look like a dunce. The story would definitely earn more sympathy from him.

Time to hit this home. She let the tears well up in her eyes.

"She does hurt us." Marit sniffed. "Our parents died not long ago, and she'd always been mean to us, but after they were gone, it got worse. Me and Hilde try be nice to her, but she won't listen. Camilla screams and slaps at us, and she pushes us around. I just want to get away. We tried to run away once, but she found out and punished us."

Marit kept her head down and pretended to wipe her eyes. "The only break we get from her is when she babysits for a rich family in town, but they fired her because she had relations with the husband."

"Go on," the troll said. What more could he want? She sure hoped her next words didn't conflict with what Hilde had said.

"It's just that Hilde is sick so much. I think it's because Camilla gives us so little food. You saw how skinny Hilde was. How skinny I am. I'm doing okay, but Hilde... sometimes she's in bed for days, and Camilla won't even let us go get the doctor. I saw her slip poison into Hilde's food once. We have to get away before she kills us. Please, Mr. Troll. Please let me go."

Marit deserved an award for her acting.

"If that's true, then you should let her pass the bridge. You need to come with me so I can keep you safe. There's another troll on the other side, and he'll kidnap you and eat you."

Another troll waiting on the other side. Nope, he wasn't fooling her.

"I promise you that she'll be a spectacular treat." Marit backed away from the troll. He didn't make a move to stop her, so she kept going. "She'll be along right behind me." This was much easier than she'd thought.

"Wait, don't—"

"Thank you." She spun around and took off running.

"Stop!" he yelled. She glanced back, scared that he was following, but he didn't. "Don't go any farther."

She was halfway across the bridge, and he was still standing there, so she continued on. The stories about this creature were so wrong. This had been way too easy.

She was almost there. Just a few steps farther. She took one look back and saw Camilla start for the bridge. She might even talk him into letting her pass too, which meant Camilla would make it to Trenten.

Hopefully, the troll was feeling hungry and would take Camilla. Either way, it didn't matter…

Marit was almost free.

Chapter Seven

Camilla trudged slowly towards the bridge. Hilde had passed by and now Marit. Now it was her turn. This was working, and she would soon be off to a new life in Trenten.

The troll hadn't moved since Marit walked away, but he stared off after her. Camilla took one step onto the bridge and froze, the stink of rotting fish surrounding her. She gulped at the sight of the troll and clutched her pack. His dirt-stained face turned towards her. He was tall but nowhere near the seven feet of the stories she'd heard.

Thick unkempt hair covered his head, and the same dark hair peeked out from under the cuffs of his sleeves and at the bottoms of his worn pants. Big, hairy feet with four toes topped by gnarled dirty toenails stood way too close to her.

"You are the last sister," the troll said.

"I am not. I have another sister behind me. See." She pointed to Tally, who still stood there with wide eyes.

"No, there is not." The gruff voice sent chills through Camilla.

"Yes, my sister Tally. She's tall and the most beautiful of us all." Camilla had to get through this and tried to slow her pounding heart.

"Your sisters have given you up to me; do you realize that?" His hand shot out, and he grabbed hold of her pack.

Camilla looked down the bridge but couldn't see her sisters on the other side because of the dense trees. "What do you mean?"

"They promised me the last sister, the third and youngest sister, would be the best."

The best. Meaning the fattest. More food for the hungry troll.

Camilla's heart sank. Hilde and Marit had never particularly loved her, but she'd never expected they'd sacrifice her to get past this beast. The emptiness crushed into her body like the charging river rapids below her.

She had no more will to fight. Her parents were gone, and her sisters betrayed her and left her to die. They'd probably planned this, and she'd gone along with their plan and was now stuck.

Running wouldn't work: he'd catch her. And she had no chance fighting the troll.

"I will go with you willingly, but I ask for one consideration."

"You are in no position to be asking for favors. You and your sisters have lied to me all along." The troll folded his long arms. "But I will listen."

Thank goodness. Maybe she could talk him out of eating her.

"Please don't eat me. Take me to your cave. I promise I will cook and clean and do anything you want. I took care of my sisters' home, and I can take care of yours too."

"I have no need for a maid." His wiry dark brown hair stuck out in every direction, and his face was half-covered with a beard. His intense blue eyes were the only beautiful thing among his foul features.

"But your clothes. I can mend them too." She eyed all the holes in his ratty trousers and his shirt that looked like it was made of burlap. "And I promise you that your home will be clean. I can sew you new clothes if you find some fabric, and I can make your dinners. Mother taught me how to cook years ago, and I love to…" Oh no, what was she getting herself into? She swallowed at the lump in her throat. "Just don't make me cook, um… people."

"Will you beat me as you did them?" the troll asked. "And will you be adding arsenic to my food too?"

Camilla took a step back. "Maybe you can eat arsenic, but that would kill us. I wouldn't even use it on a rat." She took another hard breath. "I promise to take care of your cave though or wherever you live. And I…" Her mind went blank. She had to offer something more. She had to show him she had worth.

"I can draw your picture," she blurted.

"Come again?" He rubbed at his hairy chin like he didn't understand. She was so dense. A man-eating troll living underneath the bridge would have no need for drawings.

But maybe he would appreciate it. Her drawings were good, and she improved all the time with practice.

"I can write you a story to go with it, and I can draw you a picture so you know what you look like."

The troll frowned.

Oh no. He was scary ugly, and she couldn't draw him that way. He probably wouldn't believe that was him.

He sighed, his shoulders hunched slightly. "Why don't you come with me, young lady."

"Camilla. My name is Camilla."

If he heard her name, the troll might see her as a person and not some delicious meal. She held onto that hope for now.

Chapter Eight

"We're going there." The troll pointed down the embankment that led to the river. Thankfully, he carried her pack. "Watch your step on the way down so you don't fall."

A courteous troll. He must treat people well to put them at ease before he ate them. It would make his job easier if they didn't fight, she supposed.

She put her hand on the rocky ground as she crawled down the side of the steep terrain, but he descended in front of her with little effort. Sometimes she had to sit on the rock and slide her behind down little by little. Her foot slipped once, but she caught herself.

She didn't want to die; she had to show him how valuable she could be.

By the time she reached the bottom, she was huffing and puffing. The troll, on the other hand, was breathing as normal, and her stomach turned queasy at his sour breath. She stood and shook the dust and dirt out of her skirt.

"I'm sorry for being slow. I assure you that I will keep up whatever duties you assign me."

His lip curled up as if to say something, but he remained silent. Camilla stared at the rushing water. If she knew how to swim, she'd jump right in and let the water carry her to safety, but drowning was no more desirable than being eaten.

The trees at the top of the embankment shaded her from the blazing sun, and she looked up once more, hoping this wasn't her last time seeing the blue sky and the green life of the forest.

"This way." The troll grabbed her arm, leaving a mark on her light brown shirt. She'd probably have to scrub to get his stench out, a small price to pay to avoid being eaten. She would definitely make him some new clothes. The trousers were too short, and his ragged burlap shirt looked like it might fall apart. It must not feel scratchy since he had so much hair.

He led her to a spot under the bridge and rapped on a large slab of rock with his big fist. Camilla's eyes popped open as a door shimmered into place. The troll twisted the knob and drew open the door.

"It's a little dark, but please step inside. We'll wait for our eyes to adjust, and then we'll walk down a hallway to some steps. The candles on the wall will show the way."

He nudged her inside and shut the door. A cool silence enveloped her, and she felt utterly alone. She hadn't thought this all through. She should've fought him and tried to run, but now she was at his mercy. It would be so easy for him to wrap his large hands around her neck in the dark and squeeze. He hadn't actually accepted her deal, but he'd also said he wouldn't kill her right away.

She had to stay focused and keep her wits about her.

No, he wouldn't kill her in the hall. He'd wait until they got to his home. Hopefully he'd knock her out quickly, and she wouldn't feel a thing.

"When you see the lights, you can start walking," he gruffed.

Camilla looked up and saw two straight lines of light that trailed off into the distance. She reached her hands out to the wall, but she touched something—smooth skin. An arm.

"Sorry." He jerked back.

But long brown hair covered his arms, so that couldn't be his skin.

She found the walls on each side, the small candles burning above her head. They gave off so little light but illuminated the path before her.

A glance backwards showed the troll was right behind her, but nothing was visible except his dark form.

She thought back to what he had said on the bridge when he'd questioned if she would poison him. He had asked another question, but the poison thing had thrown her.

"Did you ask me if I would try beat you?" The thought was laughable for several reasons. She could never harm a creature as big as him, but she would never do such a thing in the first place.

"Yes," he said.

"Why would you say that?"

"Because your sisters accused you of holding back food to punish them and using your fists on them."

She spun around, and he stopped short, just before stomping on her feet. She couldn't see him, but she felt the warmth of his body.

"That's silly. I would never hurt them. Why would they say that?"

But she knew why.

They were trying to gain sympathy from the troll.

Hilde and Marit were free, and they left her to be eaten. They had not wanted her to hinder their spectacular lives in Trenten even though Camilla had done far more than her share of supporting their family.

Tally could have been used as the third sister. They didn't need to sully Camilla's good name and sacrifice her to the troll.

Despite the cool air, she simmered on the inside as she stomped down the hall. She wasn't a liar or a thief or an abuser.

It wasn't fair.

She'd done everything for them with little complaint, and she'd been a decent sister; she didn't say a cruel word about others, and yet, she was the one they condemned to die.

Why couldn't they love her? Rejection would have been better than death. She sniffed, trying to clear the pressure inside her nose, and her clenched hands fell open.

"Are you okay?" The troll touched her shoulder, and she stiffened.

"I can't believe they deserted me. Did they really sacrifice me to you?"

"Yes. They said…" He paused, his voice uncertain.

"You can tell me the truth." Her shoulders slumped, and her shoes felt as if filled with mud. Every bone in her body ached from exhaustion and the weight of her pain.

He recounted the details that Hilde and Marit had told him, each story sillier than the last. It was like they took their own worst traits and used them against Camilla.

"And the reason they had to leave town was that you stole money from the school you taught at, and then that you bedded the husband of a woman you worked for."

Camilla choked out a sob and fell to her knees, hitting the stone floor. She should have never trusted them; she was as dense and gullible as they claimed, forgiving them time after time. The tears rolled off her cheeks and hit her hands.

"There, there. It'll be okay." The troll wrapped his arms around her and pulled her close. Her face rubbed up against his hard chest. She wanted to move away from him but had little effort left in her body.

He must have put on some type of cloak because his shirt was smooth like silk. Not that brown burlap he'd been wearing earlier.

"No, it's not. I'm trapped in some underground cavern by a troll who wants to eat me because I'm an ugly hog." She rubbed her thumping temples. "And then I find out my sisters lied and said I was a thief and a husband stealer and an abuser. It was them who did that."

He pushed back to his knees and grabbed her wet chin.

"My lady, you are a stunning flower in a field of weeds, and don't ever let anybody tell you differently."

His words meant a lot. She knew she wasn't ugly and that she had worth beyond being a maid, but years of her sisters' abuse often made her feel that way.

She couldn't see anything more than the outline of his head, but she felt the heat from his cheek, the sweet breath of his mouth.

Wait—sweet breath? He no longer had the stench of rotting fish or his sour breath. Now he smelled like pine trees.

"Thank you, sir." She bit down on her lip. "Um, what is your name?"

"Erik. And now you don't need to think of me as *the troll.*"

"Thank you for your kind words, Erik." Perhaps dirty trolls were attracted to less desirable women.

That was wrong. She shouldn't think of the troll—Erik—in that way. He didn't see her in such a harsh light.

Camilla's sisters might have sent her off to get killed, but she still had her dignity. She would serve Erik in whatever capacity he expected, and she would be gracious that he spared her life.

If he spared her life.

Chapter Nine

"We're coming to the stairs now. Do you see them?" Erik said.

Camilla slowed down to a stop at the end of the path. She peered down a spiral staircase winding to who knows where and shivered.

"I don't get it. We were walking forever. I mean, it seemed long. Now this staircase. How are you able to catch all those people who cross the bridge?"

"Sometimes people confuse me with my brother. He lives at the other end, and he is the troll you want to avoid."

"Oh, you're working together?" They never had a chance with two trolls. Hopefully her sisters were okay.

There she went again. After they'd sent her to her death, she was still hoping they were safe.

"We're not working together. It's a long story, and I will explain it once we arrive." He skirted Camilla and started down the steps, not even checking to see if she followed. "I know what it's like to have vile kin," he said with a touch of sadness.

Camilla's betrayers were free to make their new lives, and she would either be roasted in a huge pan or be a slave to this beast forever.

No, she kept having these scary thoughts, but he wouldn't be talking to her in such a way if he planned to eat her. She'd never given much thought to the troll other than that he was an awful creature, but yet this man had thoughts and feelings like she.

Erik remained quiet, and Camilla counted steps, but once she got to a hundred, she quit. Going down was easy, but going up would take forever.

Not that she would ever go up. Her stomach was twisted into knots. She'd never smell the fresh air after a cool rain, never see the blue eggs of a robin crack open to reveal new life. She'd never see the purples and blues and pinks and oranges of a sunset.

She'd be stuck in a cave in the ground forever.

"When we arrive, I will find you some food. Are you hungry?" Erik asked.

"Just a little. But I can make my own food, and I can prepare your meal too. I'm a talented cook. Baker especially. Bread. Do you like bread?"

"I love bread."

"Rye is my specialty, but cinnamon raisin is my favorite. Sonja even asked me if I'd come work with her at the bakery, but I couldn't quit on the Berdahls."

But that was exactly what had happened—she had left. She would miss them all and hadn't had much time to let it sink in that they were leaving for good.

"I was their maid, and they treated me well. They were always respectful and didn't take advantage like what happens to others sometimes."

She felt dense for rambling on about people he'd never met, but if he got to know her, he'd be less likely to eat her.

"Desserts," she blurted. "How about desserts? I can make anything you want."

"I've been told…" He chuckled. "That I have a slight sweet tooth."

"Then you won't like the taste of me. I sweat so much and taste of salt. I would not make a suitable meal."

He had to believe her. He must.

Erik laughed and hefted the bag higher on his shoulder. "Did you pack your recipe books in your pack?"

"No, we left most everything behind, and besides, the recipes my mother taught me are all in my head."

"Impressive."

She saw his head nod in front of her, but it was still too dark to see more than an outline of a shape from the lights marking the staircase. Living in a cave would be so dark and dreary. And damp since they were probably under the river.

Finally they reached the end. Erik did a similar knock as he'd done above, the door opened, and he stepped into the bright light of another hallway. Camilla squinted and followed.

Erik stood in front of her, and she blinked, trying to get used to the light. No, that wasn't Erik.

The man standing before her wore a red silk shirt rolled up to his elbows, and his long black hair was tied at the nape of his neck with a matching ribbon. This man was handsome, with a chiseled face and strong blue eyes.

Eyes that looked eerily similar to the troll's.

"Are you getting used to the light?" he asked, a smirk on his face.

But that was the voice of Erik.

"Where did…" She grabbed his arm, touching the smooth silk she'd felt earlier. "What's going on?"

"I apologize for being mysterious, but I'm afraid if I'd tried to explain above, you wouldn't have believed me. Walk with me."

He stepped away, and she hurried to catch up, her eyes on his broad shoulders and tanned skin. No more wild hair, no ragged clothing, no hairy feet.

"Years ago, an angry witch cursed our family. Any time I go up to the surface, my body changes into what you saw above. Down here is the only place I can be me."

"What did you do?" Camilla asked.

"Nothing. It was wrongs committed long before I was born, before my grandfather even." Erik came to a dead-end and again did his special knock on the wall. He held the door open, and she peered through.

A sea of trees lay before her, a forest underneath the ground. A hawk swooped around the giant oaks like the ones in her yard that reached up to the... She gazed up to an azure sky.

"How is this possible? We're so far underground."

"That's the magic of my world. Welcome to Escavia."

"Are the trees real?" She ran to the nearest tree and pulled off a leaf. Her finger rubbed the smooth face.

"They're real."

She blushed. "May I get something from my bag please?" She wanted to wipe the sheen of sweat from her forehead.

He handed her the pack, and she dug inside, dumping a few things out until she found the small cloth. She knelt on the lush grass and wiped her forehead.

When she turned back to him, she froze. He was looking at the book with all her stories of the men who had romanced her.

"You have been a busy woman." He smirked.

"They're not real. Just fantasies."

She felt like she'd fallen into a new world. Her fear had all but disappeared, replaced with the feeling deep inside that Erik would not cause her any harm.

"These are marvelous. Did you draw them?" He studied the page and continued to flip on.

"Yes. They get a little better as you go along."

"Look at the detail. I can read the emotions on her face. She looks sad."

Camilla glanced at the picture—it was a self-portrait, one of the few included in the book. She had been the character in her stories, but the women she drew didn't always look as she did. But the portrait was her.

"She is sad." Heartache had filled Camilla's last few years, ever since her parents died.

Erik stuffed the book back into her pack. "Well, you are quite the artist. Have you done any paintings?"

"No. I don't have money to buy those things. Just a book and a pencil is what I can afford. I enjoy drawing though. It relaxes me. Even if my stories are silly."

"The world needs silly stories." He smiled and walked to a trail that headed into the woods. She took a deep breath and followed after, making note of his silk shirt and fancy trousers. Even his shoes appeared to be fine leather.

The path curved around through the trees, and the sunlight filtered through the leafy canopy. They came to a small stream, and Erik turned. Camilla was close enough to see the stubble on his face and his strong nose.

He was more handsome than Oskar, more handsome than any man she'd seen.

"Climb on my back. I'll carry you across so you don't get wet."

She laughed. "No, I can walk."

"Pish posh. You'll get your feet wet, and there's no reason to soak both of us. Why don't you hold your pack." He held out the bag, and she took it. "Now, climb on."

He turned his back to her and waited. She was much too big for him to carry. He would stumble and fall.

"Am I too tall?" He knelt down and turned his head. "What's wrong?"

"You can't carry me."

Something flickered in his eyes, sorrow. And the way he was looking at her, she almost thought he could see into her soul.

"You are not. You're perfect."

She scoffed. "Are all the women in your world my size?"

"No." He chuckled. "They're the same as women above ground. Some tiny, some huge, and everything in between. You have beautiful curves and a truly wonderful smile."

He laughed at her red face and stood. Quickly, he scooped her up into his arms. Before she argued, he rushed off into the water. It wasn't very deep, only up past his knees, and he made it across quickly.

He set her down gently. "See, I told you I could carry you. I'm not even breaking a sweat."

"That's because you were walking through cold water." She allowed herself a smile.

They followed the stream for a short time. The noise of crashing water assaulted her ears, and she smelled the moisture in the air. A waterfall?

She ran ahead and stopped when she got to the edge. The water fell a hundred feet down a cliff, and she gazed out over a city that went on for as far as she could see. People and horses and carts filled the streets next to buildings that were three and four windows high. It was just as she'd imagined Trenten to be.

"That is Escavia." Erik laid his hand on her shoulder.

"It's amazing. And so huge. I never knew such a place existed."

"Not many people do, and for a reason. This is where I bring the people I rescue."

"Rescue?"

"Yes. I told you how my family was cursed and how my brother lies in wait at the other end of the bridge. He is the one who steals people from above. I try to help them. Any person attempting to cross is given a choice. Come here to Escavia or continue at their own risk to face Shelton."

"But why don't you help them get past him?"

"I can't. I can only make it about halfway, and an invisible chain holds me back. We have an exit down here that goes to the other side of the river, but people need to trust me first. And well, you remember how I looked and the stories you've heard."

"They think you're trying to trick them so you can eat them." She had thought the same thing, had made judgments about him because of how he looked.

"Most believe that to be true. Some choose to come with me, bargaining as you did." He gave her a cheeky smile, and she blushed. Luckily, the mist from the waterfall peppered her face, cooling her down.

"That was pretty silly."

Wait—Hilde and Marit. They crossed the bridge.

"Did Shelton get my sisters? Are they…"

"Probably." He nodded grimly. "Nobody passes by Shelton and lives to tell."

"But did you tell them about him?"

"Yes, but they didn't believe me. They were too busy trying to convince me to take you. I tried so very hard—I always do, and I always give the person the choice."

"You didn't give *me* a choice?"

He laughed. "You didn't let me. You volunteered to come down right away." Erik scratched his chin, his face serious. "It's hard for me sometimes too, to know what I look like and how I scare people. I know what they think of me above, all because of Shelton."

"But how did he become evil?" Did most of the people continue on, or did many come down here? She had so many questions.

"His choices. He was never the nicest guy, and then he stayed above ground too long, and well… Here we are."

"So I can leave whenever I want?"

"You would be brought to the surface through another door, and we would send you on your way. Or you can go back from where you came. Shelton would not be a danger to you as long as you don't cross back over the bridge."

She had two choices: return home to the scorn of those who hated her sisters or go on to Trenten to a place where she knew nobody. Neither option seemed like a good one. At least here, she had Erik to advise her.

She didn't speak, and Erik continued. "You are also welcome to stay. There are those who are looking to hire, and you could work for them instead of being my personal slave."

Camilla let out a laugh. He must have thought she was so silly, bowing down before him and begging him to enslave her.

"So you're not hiring any maids now, I suppose."

Erik chuckled. "Not at the moment. If…" His face fell serious. "If you are as good at baking as you claim, I could put in a word for you at one of our many bakeries."

He grinned, and the gratitude filled her. He had done so much for her already, and she wasn't sure how she could ever thank him.

"I would appreciate that." Maybe she could find someone fun to work with like Sonja. "So how about you show me around Escavia. I'd really love to see your lands."

"Your wish is my command." He bowed and offered his arm, which she grabbed willingly.

Chapter Ten

Marit had waited until she saw the troll take Camilla before she hit the very end of the bridge. She should feel guilty, but this was the right thing. Camilla never would survive in a city like Trenten.

She stepped over that last part of the bridge. Just around the trees Hilde would be waiting.

Something struck her chest, and she flew backwards. Her head slammed into the ground. She grabbed it to try and stem the pain. No blood thankfully, but she felt the rocks ingrained in her skull.

A shadow passed across her face, and she opened her eyes. The troll stood over her, his breath dank and rancid.

"Ahh, a second treat," he said. He sounded different than before. And how could he get to this side so quickly when he'd just taken Camilla? The troll offered his hand. "Let me help you up, my dear."

He grasped her wrist and jerked her to her feet. "Ouch," she squealed. He let go, and she dusted off her skirt and her hair. Her head still throbbed. "You took

Camilla." She spun around to look back but saw nothing.

It could be magic. She'd never considered that a troll might have dark magic. They were just ugly creatures who lived by rivers.

"You must be mistaken." He laughed darkly. "I presume you're speaking of my brother."

"Your brother?" The words caught in Marit's throat.

"Yes, my idiot brother. The one who tries to steal away my delicious treats. Let me introduce myself. I am Shelton."

The fear crept into Marit's soul, and she looked the troll over. He had the same build and hairy body as the other, except instead of eyes of blue, this one had eyes as dark as the muddy water beneath the bridge. She tightened her grip on her pack and checked the distance to the end, which was now farther away.

"Where's my sister?" she said with a shaky voice.

"Ahh, you want to see your sister." His gaze ran up and down her body, and he licked his lips. "Let me lead the way."

He grabbed her roughly. She almost stumbled, but somehow managed to regain her footing. This was a mistake. She had to get away.

"Um, I'll talk to her later." Marit tugged, trying to loosen his grip, but he was too strong.

"Sorry, beautiful. You're coming with me now." He pulled her towards the embankment.

"Please let me go. I have a third sister. She'll be right behind me. She's fat and will provide you with a full meal. I'll go get her and make sure she comes down. I promise I'll bring her back."

She struggled to get loose as the troll's sinister laughter surrounded her. His grip was like a cuff she couldn't escape. She kicked at him, and he swore.

Suddenly, she was flying through the air and landed on his broad shoulders. He held down her legs with one arm, and she pounded on his back, trying to wiggle and worm her way out of his clutches, but he hardly flinched. She yanked at his stringy hair, but he tilted his head to the side, and the greasy strands slipped through her fingers, his laughter increasing.

Tears flooded her face and fell onto his shoulder as he climbed down the embankment like it was nothing, never once teetering. He reached the river's edge and stretched his arm out and swiped the rock in front of them.

A door flashed into view, and they stepped into a small hallway.

"Money, I can give you money," Marit choked out.

"I have no need for money."

Marit shuddered, knowing what she had to do. She didn't want to imagine him running his rough and hairy hands over her body, but she had no choice. "I promise to have relations with you if you release me."

He snorted and threw her down. She rubbed the spot on her butt that had hit the ground.

"I'm not interested. All I want is my dinner."

"Please," she sobbed. "Please let me go." How was she going to get away? She looked towards the door they'd come through, but it had disappeared, leaving a blank wall. She had to pull herself together, or she would die.

He dragged her across the threshold of another door and released her.

Marit looked around the room—a parlor with a sofa and pillows and a shelf full of books. This was the home of a normal person, someone she could reason with.

The troll grabbed her hair and jerked her to her feet. She squealed in pain, but he laughed. "Let's go."

He grasped her shoulder and thrust her forward. They marched through the room into a gleaming kitchen with a giant black oven and a large icebox the size only the rich had. A number of pots and pans hung along the wall along with utensils she'd never seen, and he had shelves of bagged foods and spices.

She took a deep breath of the heavenly smell. It had to be coming from that oven. Camilla was a decent cook, but rarely did she fill their home with such decadent smells.

"What are you making?" She needed to distract him so she could think about what she would do.

"It's crème brûlée."

"Oh, I love crème brûlée. It's one of my favorites." It wasn't. She'd eaten it, and it was disgusting.

He stared at her like he knew she was lying, but then he smiled. "Well then, perhaps you should join me for dinner."

This might work. He was probably trying to throw her off with the whole *I'm not interested in relations* thing. Marit grabbed his arm and fluttered her eyes up at him in that way men loved.

"And how about some akevitt for dinner?" She strained to avoid reacting to his stench—she couldn't make him mad now.

"Definitely akevitt," he agreed.

"This is a beautiful kitchen." She pretended to admire the room but studied the big metal door built into the wall. What in the world was that for? Did he lock away his food supplies so nobody stole them?

"It's functional," he said. "I do what I can in here." The troll took out a bottle of akevitt and set it on the counter. Marit could get him drunk and then escape.

The troll leaned on his hands and grinned at her. "You're dirty, my dear. Why don't you go take a bath and clean up. You'll find a robe on the back of the door."

Ah-ha. He did want to have relations with her. He would draw her out in her bathrobe and find an excuse for her to remove it. He must be shy, afraid to take that next step with her, but that was okay. She could take control and show him what to do.

She just hoped he would take a bath too.

After they finished, he'd let her go, and she'd be on her way to Trenten. Hilde was probably there. This had been a ruse to get her to have relations with him.

Marit knew men, and despite him being a troll, he was still a man underneath, and if he was as big as the rest of his body, he would satisfy her greatly. She would just have to plug her nose from the stench.

She put on her best seductive smile. "Show me where I can clean up."

Chapter Eleven

Camilla stood at the outskirts of the city, gazing at the wonder before her. A bustling market with people and booths of wares filled the park, and wonderful smelling foods wafted in the air.

"How many people live here?" she asked.

"About fifteen thousand."

My word that was a lot of people, more even than Trenten.

A man walked up the sidewalk to Erik and Camilla and gave them a quick bow.

"Hello, Ephram," Erik said. "How are your daughter and her new husband?"

"Terrific, sir. They are settling in."

"Good to hear. Say hello to the missus for me."

"Will do, have a lovely day." Ephram waved, and they continued on their way.

Erik didn't enter the market but chose a quiet path that led along the outskirts of the park. They reached a garden filled with peas and carrots and beans and so many other vegetables. She breathed in the fresh dirt smell.

"Isn't that beautiful," Camilla said. "I've always wanted a garden, but the ground around our home was only good for pine trees."

Hilde had called her a slug once, for wanting to play in the dirt. Her sisters' betrayal had buried Camilla's remorse over their loss, but it wouldn't go away.

She was on her own now in a new place, and she had no idea where to start or what to do. How did she find a job or a place to live?

Erik leaned up against the fence and stared towards the vegetables. "I have a huge garden at home. It's so large, we have help taking care of it, but you're welcome to dig in our soil."

She grasped the fence railing and studied the black soil. "I might kill everything. I don't have much experience growing things although I talk big."

"I'm sure it'd be fine." His intense stare made her nervous.

"So, um what will I do now? I think I might want to stay a while, but I need a place to live and a job. But I know nothing about your town. It's so overwhelming."

"I know of some available rooms."

"But I have no money to pay for rent."

"I will pay the rent until you're able to start a job. We have a thriving city, and I'm sure it'll be no problem for you."

"I... I shouldn't..." She couldn't take his charity.

"Yes, you should."

"No, I can work for you and—"

"I seem to remember you offering me a drawing or two. How about you do a portrait of me. I would love that."

A picture wasn't worth what he was offering. It would take a month or so before she earned any money, but no matter how much she argued, he would tell her not to worry.

She would repay him for his generosity one day.

"I can do that. Do you really know someone who has a bakery?"

"Yes, and I'm sure you'll fit in well there."

He was talking like she already had the job. She needed to think positive like him and trust that things would work out.

They continued their walk, passing by a few people who greeted them with bows.

"Everyone is so polite here. Much different than home."

A carriage roared down the road and stopped, and a little man hopped out and ran up to the pair.

"Sir, why didn't you send a message? We would've come to pick you up." The man wiped his brow and took a big breath.

"I was enjoying a walk with my lady friend. She is new to our town."

The man straightened up and offered his hand. "Oh yes, good day, m'lady. Corwin Cobbles at your service."

"Nice to meet you." Camilla gave him a curtsey. It just felt right.

"Did the prince rescue you from the bridge?" Corwin asked.

"What prince?"

Corwin's eyes narrowed, and his head slowly tilted to the side. One brow raised high above the other, and he looked to Erik.

Camilla gasped. Prince? Erik was a prince. She should've known.

But how would she have known? And to think she'd thought he was some ugly troll when she first met him. She shuffled back under Corwin's scrutiny.

"Her confusion would be my fault. I never explained exactly who I was." Erik squeezed her arm lightly. "Why don't we hop in with Corwin now. It's a long way to the castle."

Her throat dried. "Is that where I'm staying?"

"Until we get you settled into your own place." He laughed at her shocked face. "For now, you are my guest."

Erik helped her into the carriage, and soon the buildings and people were passing by. She'd never been in a carriage before, and it seemed to be so much faster than the wagon her parents had before they died.

The city held so much she wanted to explore, so many people to meet, but her mind kept going back to the man with her. A prince rescued her and was taking her to his castle.

Her sisters were troll food, and she was saved by a prince.

Erik's eyes flickered to the window, and she followed his gaze. They came around the side of another park, and the castle appeared before her. She gripped the window ledge, trying to take the whole view in.

The azure sky framed the brown brick castle with four long rows of windows and a fifth row that seemed to be built into the roof. Grand stone steps lined by flowers led up to a gigantic wooden door, and two large towers flanked each corner, with domed roofs and spires that reached for the clouds.

The bright sun seemed to hover over the grounds, bathing the green trees dotting the lush grass along with flower garden after flower garden.

It was magnificent.

"This is your home?" she asked as a small group of people on horses came around the stables off to the side.

"Many people live here."

"And is there a queen and a king?"

He laughed. "My father, yes. Although he's been sick for a while and has mostly retired from duties. My mother died about three years ago." His eyes took on a sorrow not there a moment ago. She must have been special in his life.

"I'm so sorry. My parents died a few years ago too. I miss them a lot." She placed her hand on his and squeezed. "Sometimes I think things are getting better, but then it all hits me again."

"It seems you have lost a lot too. At least I have my father and the rest of my family." He grew silent and stared off towards the riders on the horses. His smile returned. "I also have four younger brothers—not counting Shelton, and three sisters."

"My word, that is a big family. I'd always wanted brothers." Maybe if she'd had two brothers instead, her life would have been different.

"Very. Because I've got many cousins and aunts and uncles around too."

"And everybody lives in the castle?"

"No." He laughed. "Only my immediate family, but the royal staff lives on the grounds."

"I'm staying in a castle tonight," she whispered to herself, and he laughed.

The carriage stopped at the bottom of the steps to the main entrance. Erik helped her out, and a minute later, she walked through the doors to a castle... a real castle.

If only her sisters could see her now.

A small bit of guilt flowed through her, but she shut it off. They had made their choices.

Erik and Camilla barely got through the door and were accosted by people with questions for the prince. He took command of the group, responding to some questions and promising answers to others later, and just as soon as they'd flocked to Erik, they disappeared.

"Now," Erik said, grasping her hands. "I have two options. I can show you to your room so you can take a little rest, or I can give you a tour of the castle."

"A tour," she blurted.

He chuckled. "Fantastic. That's what I was hoping you'd say."

Erik led her through the castle, stopping at different rooms to explain their use, putting up with her silly questions along the way. Every once in a while, they passed some people, and Erik always introduced her.

In the kitchen, a woman presented Erik with a picnic basket. A young boy about six ran through the door at full speed and skidded to a stop in front of Erik.

"When did you get back? Are we going on a picnic?"

Erik laughed and motioned to the three of them standing there. "*We* are not going on a picnic." He pointed to just himself and Camilla. "*We* are."

"Ahhh." The boy frowned.

"Nathanial, meet my friend Camilla." He laid his hand on her shoulder. "He is my little brother."

"I'm not little anymore. I'm growing." Nathanial crossed his arms, his blonde hair falling into his eyes.

"No kidding. I noticed you put on some muscle. Keep at it, and soon you'll be bigger than Jules."

Nathanial smiled.

"Camilla and I haven't had a chance to talk much, so we're going to eat alone, but we'll be at dinner tonight, and perhaps you can have the job of introducing her to everyone."

"I can?" His eyes opened wide.

Camilla swallowed hard. She would be meeting the royal family, all at once. Erik was one thing, but the king and all his sons and daughters would be studying her, wondering who she was and why she was there.

"You can." He patted Nathanial on the head, and the boy took off for the door.

"I'm telling Jules," he yelled.

"This may be overwhelming." Erik grabbed her hand and squeezed. "But you'll be fine. My family is very welcoming."

"Do you always bring the people you rescue back to the castle?"

"No. Only the young and beautiful ladies." He winked. "And I'm afraid not many of them can be talked into joining us down here at Escavia."

He took the picnic basket in one arm and held on to her hand as he led her out of the kitchen. They headed down a hall and through a door to more steps.

Out in the backyard, he laid out a blanket, and they settled onto the ground. Camilla smelled the sweet scent of flowers again and searched for the source. She spotted the small flower garden bursting with colors across the yard.

"I don't get it. The sun is shining, but we're underground. How does this all work? How do all these buildings fit underground? Where does their air come from?"

She ran her hand over the soft green grass, so unlike the scratchy grass around her home.

Erik laughed, unpacking the food. "It's magic. The sun here follows the same schedule as the one above ground." His face grew serious. "I'm sorry you were forced to join us down here."

"I'm not," Camilla said quickly. She really hadn't had a chance to think about it all.

"Crossing the bridge is impossible. Shelton stops anyone who tries, and this is their only option to stay alive, to come down here for their safe passage."

"But how do you get back there? How do you get to the people in time before Shelton?" Many people must have been caught because Erik was unable to get to the bridge in time.

"It's part of the magic, the curse, which hit me when I turned eighteen. So if I suddenly disappear, I apologize, but when someone steps onto the bridge, I am whisked away. It's not just me, but I have one other brother who it happens to also. Bjarne turned eighteen this past year, and now I have help."

Camilla had never thought magic was real, and it was hard to understand what he was saying.

"So the same thing happened to Shelton, but he went to the other side and was bad?"

"That is the short version." He shrugged helplessly. "He is a year younger than me and has been terrorizing people for almost four years now."

"But the troll has been there for decades." Wreaking havoc on those poor travelers.

"It's a family curse, and unfortunately we have some bad apples going down our line too."

Camilla smoothed her skirt over her knees. A curse was the reason so many people died. That and people who couldn't see through Erik's rough exterior.

"So, will you stay with us here or continue on to Trenten?" he asked.

"There's nothing there for me."

"I'm glad. I think I'll like having a new friend around here."

The smile Erik gave her made her insides tingle. It was too much to think that a prince could be interested in her, but he wanted to be her friend.

She glanced up at a cardinal flying overhead. This world was just like hers, and she would be very happy here.

Erik handed her a plate with chicken, sliced apples, and salad. "I'm sorry your first dinner here isn't fancier."

She laughed. This meal was more than enough, more than she'd ever imagined.

"No, it's just what I want. It's perfect."

Chapter Twelve

Marit finished showering and dried off with the lush towel. She could get used to this. Maybe she'd have to sneak one out when she left.

A knock sounded on the door. "Wear your hair up," the troll said.

"I will," Marit replied. She searched through the drawers and found a small string, so she did a quick braid and made a bun, tucking her hair in as best as she could.

She eyed her smooth curves in the mirror. The troll wouldn't say no to her—no man could. The red silk robe hung on the hook, exactly where he had said. She slipped it on, and it dragged on the floor. She'd have to leave it cracked open to give him a peek.

Marit exited the bathroom and found the troll with a glass of akevitt in his hand.

"Do you have one for me?" she said with a sly grin.

He stood and stepped over to her, his stench following. He stuck his nose close to her neck and sniffed in deeply. "Fresh and clean," he said.

"Of course." Marit spread apart the top of the robe to show more skin, but he didn't seem to notice. She should suggest to him that a bath was a marvelous idea, but she didn't want to offend him. She would just have to suffer through it.

"Follow me, my dear." The troll led her to the kitchen.

Marit stopped outside the doorway. A huge cast iron pot sat on the counter, a jar of brown liquid next to it. The light bounced off the two pairs of metal cuffs. She stiffened, closing the gap in the robe and tightening the strap. She didn't want to be tied up when he bedded her.

"Are we going to eat first?" her shaky voice asked, gaze focused on the cuffs.

"Yes, dinner. I'm hungry, and I hate to wait, but I have little choice." The troll glanced from Marit to a red dessert sitting on the table. "I guess I'll enjoy my dessert first. I'm sure she's quite tasty."

Marit's heart thumped in her head. Crème brûlée was yellow. His was deep red... blood red.

"Where's my sister?" Her voice trembled.

"Don't you worry about her." He smirked as he stepped towards Marit, his hands outstretched. She backed up until she hit the door. His arms pinned her, and she couldn't move—couldn't get free.

"No," she squealed.

The troll laughed, his putrid breath washing over her as he removed her robe. He tossed it onto a chair and grabbed her wrist to pull her towards the counter. She twisted, clawing for the counter that was too far away, but he was too strong, and she slid across the floor.

In one quick motion, he grabbed the cuffs and slapped them on her wrists behind her back. Then he dropped to the floor and cuffed her ankles.

"Please don't. I'll do anything," she begged, the tears filling her eyes. She would die, and it was all Hilde's fault.

He lifted her like she was a feather and placed her in the deep black pot. She splashed into an oily watery mix that chilled her skin, and the fear exploded.

She'd wanted to be an actress—she would've been famous. She would've found the man of her dreams and been rich, and now she would be food for a troll.

He snapped her wrist cuffs to chains attached to one side of the pot and her feet onto the other. Her body hung suspended between the two sides, submerged from her chest to her knees. She squirmed around, twisting her arms and legs, but only managed to splash the brown liquid into her eyes. Then he poured some other oily liquid over her shoulders.

Marit wailed, the pain escaping from deep in her soul. She didn't want to die.

The troll strolled over to the thick black door in the wall, grabbed the metal ring, and opened it up. A whoosh of thick steam pushed its way out of the opening.

Red hot flames licked the top of the oven, performing a morbid dance. The heat from the door smothered Marit, and she couldn't breathe.

"No, no, no!" she screamed, but the troll picked the pot up and effortlessly headed for the door.

Chapter Thirteen

Shelton peered at the girl who struggled in his pot as he carried her away.

"I've increased the heat so you'll cook a little faster. I'm starving." He shoved Marit into the oven and shut the door. She screamed and screamed and screamed, but it wouldn't take too long, and she'd quiet down.

He strode back to the counter and took another look at his dessert. *Not yet,* he reminded himself. He could wait until the main dish was done before he enjoyed his delicious treat.

Sisters. He wondered if they'd taste similar.

He refilled his glass of akevitt and went into the parlor to wait, humming an energetic tune.

This is going to be the perfect meal, he thought.

The End

Acknowledgments

Okay, it's short this time, but...

Thank you to Theresa Paolo for helping me with this story. And thank you to all those who are reading my stories. You don't know how much I appreciate it.

About the Author

Reading has always been a big part of Suzi's life. She even won the most-pages-read award a few times in her junior high English class, many years ago. She started several writing projects as a kid but never actually finished anything, and then she took a big break from writing that lasted well into adulthood.

She's written in a variety of genres, including horror, suspense, and women's fiction, and has even dipped into fantasy slightly with her fairy tale retellings. She also writes young adult stories under the name Suzi Drew.

Her non-writing life includes her family and friends, her sweet and fluffy dog, and an awesome job editing fiction with some of her writer friends. (Oh wait, that's still a part of writing. Seems she can't get away from the written word!)

To find out more about Suzi,
go to.SuziWieland.com

Also by Suzi Wieland

Please visit SuziWieland.com
for more information.

Milton Keynes UK
Ingram Content Group UK Ltd.
UKHW031156251124
451529UK00001B/10

9 798330 474578